SOFT TARGETS

CARSON WINTER

Cover & Illustrations by Blacky Shepherd
Edited by Alex Woodroe

Soft Targets *contains graphic depictions of gun violence in the workplace; caution recommended. More information is available at the end of this book.*

TENEBROUS

PRESS

Production of this novel was made possible in part by a grant from the Regional Arts & Culture Council. Visit https://racc.org/ for more information.

Published by Tenebrous Press.
Visit our website at www.tenebrouspress.com.

First Printing, March 2023.

Print ISBN: 979-8-9859923-4-2
eBook ISBN: 979-8-9859923-5-9

Cover art and interior illustrations by Blacky Shepherd.

Jacket design by Matt Blairstone.

Edited by Alex Woodroe.

Formatting by Lori Michelle.

Printed in the United States of America.

For everyone who's assaulted daily by dopamine—
or its sad absence.

1

IOFTEN THINK about what would happen if a gunman entered our building and started blasting away. I think we all do, it's like a horror movie that way. Because really, it's not enough to see it on TV. You have to duck under a table, hide in a cupboard, throw a coffee mug, and eventually feel the hot bullet spill your hot blood onto the company carpet. That's what it takes, I think, to really give a shit about what the news anchors say. No talking head is enough. It's just one of those things—the ultimate *you had to be there*, you know?

Me and Ollie knew this better than anyone, and that's why we always took our lunches together, out in his car, to just talk like a couple of kids. You know an Ollie, wherever you work. He's cool. Short, messy hair, glasses. Funny. He doesn't threaten you as a man. He won't tell anyone if you came in hungover. He won't make a big deal about your anythings if you don't make a big deal about his anythings.

We were drinking sodas in his car on an insufferable Tuesday—killing our lunchbreak with the same vigor that we killed ourselves.

"So, what happens if there's two of them?" he asked.

"What do you mean?"

"You know, two dudes with guns and they kick down the door and they go on either side of the office and they start with Melanie at the front desk and accounting on the other side. You're stuck between a rock and a hard place, my man. Hard fucking place."

"You think you can break those windows? Not with your hands, but like a chair or a stapler, or something?"

Ollie thought for a moment, rubbing his chin. "Yeah, maybe. I could see that happening. Let's say you can break the window with the—uh, uh—with the copier. Yeah, you can bash it to bits with the copier."

"I think I'd try to jump through the window, then."

"Really? Damn." He whistled. "That's tough shit. That's action hero shit. You think you're not going to hurt your leg?"

"Tuck and roll, that's what they say to do, right?"

"Yeah, but man, that's like out of a moving train or something. This is two stories up, hombre. You're gonna shatter your kneecaps."

"Better than a bullet, though, right?"

"That may be. You're saying the risk is worth the reward. You might be able to get interviewed after. 'Dude who left his co-workers to die by two gunmen speaks on the benefit of crutches.'"

I laughed. "Yeah, that's right. But I'm alive and they're dead. So, who really gives a shit?"

Ollie nodded, mugging as if I'd just revealed some deeper truth on human existence. "Very true, my friend." He toasted me with a bottle of soda as an alarm chimed from his pocket. Ollie reached down, killing the alarm. "Back to work," he said.

We both groaned.

Really, part of the problem was that our job was boring as shit. Not in the normal way, the *all jobs suck* way—our jobs were literal tedium. We, Ollie and I, both worked in data entry, meaning we entered raw data into a spreadsheet all day while silently hoping someone would come in and kill us all.

This whole fantasy was a sort of bonding factor for us. It had to be, because around us, everyone else would say shit like, "Well, it's a living!" or "At least I've got a job!"

I didn't know about them, but I did it because I couldn't

do anything else. I'd given up on finding something to do with my degree and this was a last resort until my dream job sat on my lap, shook its ass, and told me it loved me. Ollie wasn't quite in the same boat. I always assumed he was, until one day he told me that he had freelance assignments to do. After that, I managed to put it together—Ollie made most of his money elsewhere, but stayed on doing data entry as a means to keep health insurance. I didn't ask much about that. He would call in a lot and I knew that, because for me to be able to withstand the work day, I needed Ollie to be there to liven me up. Needless to say, every day he wasn't there was pure pain.

I figured he had an auto-immune disease or something, some sort of chronic illness. But nothing too serious, a pain in the ass that he didn't talk about, nothing he'd want you to worry about. He was young and vital, normal. Sort of.

All that bullshit about this place being a stepping stone to better things just about killed us both though, we weren't like that at all. We couldn't be fooled into thinking our situation was anything other than pure shit. So, we talked about it. A lot. And that bothered some people, because not everyone can appreciate open-hearted pessimism. Some of them needed to pretend that it was okay, that life was fair, and that hard work paid off. Over time, we began to see ourselves as distinct from the others, and soon the others left us entirely alone. Left to our own devices, our jokes got darker, more pointedly cruel. Our fantasies showed their ugly heads and I think it was me, one day, who saw on the news that some office workers got blown apart by their colleague, and I smirked and said, "Lucky bastards."

This prompted a gut-busting laugh from Ollie, of course, who had tears in his eyes when he thought about it. Just imagine, everyone around you was preparing vigils, all sad and sure that you would've wanted to live, but there you were: it was a fucking Monday and you were sure that nothing in your life had ever been right; you were working a bullshit job you hated and it was only eleven and you knew that somehow, you had to last till 6 'o clock, because they added an extra hour to the workday; you were sitting there at your desk, brain dead and tired and depressed and suddenly—*voila!*—the answer to your prayers; Craig with the AR-15 came barging in, the timid little nerd from sales all done up in tactical gear, and that motherfucker might as well have looked like an angel. "Take me, St. Craig—blow my fucking brains out or else I'll have to be here for seven more fucking hours." And Craig, the messiah figure he was, granted your wish.

It started like that; we'd talk about all the shootings that happened. Analyze their methods and motivations. We'd place ourselves both within the role of survivor and antagonist.

But, I should be clear here—this wasn't idolatry. What attracted us to the topic was the taboo that surrounded it. We liked the way others would wince when we brought up wanting to be gunned down in the parking lot. It was just a bit of dark humor, really. People said, "Kill me," all the time, right? We just took it a bit further, made it more specific. We made trite hyperbole topical again. And, of course, this made us pariahs. But what could you expect, really?

But that was survival, for both parties. This was how we sublimated our brainless work into something we could at least joke about. It gave us something to look forward to.

So, yeah, I started it all, I guess. That part was on me.

"Really? Damn." Ollie whistled. "That's tough shit. That's action hero shit."

2

OLLIE WAS A mysterious guy, but I accepted his mystery just as I accepted that snakes went *somewhere* during the winter and it wasn't my business to know where. He was constantly busy, doing one thing or another, and when he invited me over, there was a distinct feeling that his schedule, miraculously, had been cleared.

"Come in, come in," he said, exhaling. "It's been a fucking week. Don't mind the mess. These apartments collect clutter like nobody's business." Ollie always seemed to be conspicuously aware of the fact he lived in an apartment and frequently brought it up, as if he were apologizing. Sometimes, he'd go further still, and say he was saving for a house, too. I just shrugged. His place was fine, it looked like every other single dude's apartment I'd ever been to. It was a little sparse, but not in a mechanical minimalist sort of way. Things just seemed to be spaced far apart. And Ollie was also aware of this too, and also anxious about what it said about him as a person. So, sometimes the "saving for a house" comment would also reach over and cover the "why I don't have a ton of shit" question.

Again though, I didn't care. Ollie's place was painfully normal, but maybe for a guy like Ollie, that was the problem.

"Go ahead and take a seat," he said. He disappeared into the kitchenette and came back with two beers. "You still like garbage beer, right?"

"Always have, always will."

He tossed me a can. "Maybe don't open that right away."

I licked the dew from my fingers and sat the beer down in front of me. Ollie sat beside me and we watched junk television and bullshitted for a couple of hours. About life, girls in the office, job openings, and whatever else came to mind. I didn't usually broach the subject of Ollie's freelance work, because, I guess, for me, it felt something like an invasion of privacy. He'd never mentioned it before in more than passing, so I figured he didn't want to talk about it. And that was it. But his laptop was sitting on the table and the words sort of just popped out: "So, how's the side hustle going?"

I didn't think Ollie would be surprised or annoyed or anything. He's not the type to get up in arms about something like that. Still, I felt a little like I was needling into something I had no business needling into.

But Ollie just laughed. "Less than bueno," he said.

I felt bad for asking. Maybe his insecurity about his apartment was also a reflection of his finances. "Sorry, dude," I mustered, then tried to relieve the tension I felt with a joke. "If you ever need a place to stay, I have a couch covered in dried Hot Pocket guts."

"Does it come with amenities?"

"Just a trash can that never stops smelling because the lid's broken."

"Well, gee," he said, deadpan. "I'll put down a deposit tomorrow."

We laughed a bit, riffing on the idea of living together, but then slowly, throughout the night, the whole idea transformed into something that didn't feel so much like a joke. We were each a six-pack deep and Ollie had brought out what he called, "the paraphernalia," and we were both now holding in lungfuls of weed smoke. When we released, we both simultaneously fell backwards into his couch.

"Okay, but what about this—instead of me moving into

your place, or you moving into my place—what if we got a place together?"

"How's that gonna look?"

"Like we're a couple."

"Well, if that's the case, we should definitely do it."

He made a *cheers* motion with his beer. "But, check this, some quick math. So, our apartments, individually, are one bedroom shit holes, right?"

"Yes, agreed."

"Now, a two bedroom shit hole is, on average, only what a one bedroom costs plus a couple hundred dollars."

"Sure," I said, although I thought that sounded low.

"So, what do you pay now? A thousand a month?"

"I prefer to call it a 'k,' but yes."

"So, two bedrooms is only about $1200 a month. But that's a shit hole, we don't want a shit hole, so how do we transition from shit hole to semi-decent and livable? Tack on another couple hundred bucks, motherfucker!"

"Fourteen-hundred," I said, already knowing where he was going.

"No, not $1400, but $700. Because we split the rent. And that means two things: we each now have an extra $300 a month, to do whatever we want with. Invest in crypto, build wealth, save it, spend it, develop a pill habit, who cares? And two, we have a better living space, which will benefit our mental health and make us infinitely more fuckable."

"Well, only if we can convince anyone we bring home that we aren't fucking each other."

"Hey, man—why grab a hamburger when you have steak at home?" We laughed about that a bit and smoked more and drank more and diverted our conversations around and around and around, until Ollie, his eyes red and nearly glued shut, said, "Seriously, man. Just think about it."

"I will, I will," I promised. And why not? I liked Ollie. We kept each other sane. And somehow, this was all making sense. But also, I expected it to be forgotten in the morning, when we both went to work, and fell into the same rhythm of malaise we always did.

Except, that didn't happen at all.

The morning after, I'd gotten to my desk before Ollie and I was really praying that he hadn't called in sick, because I was going to have a rough nine hours otherwise. But, to my surprise, he came in just a couple minutes after me, holding something.

"Morning, beautiful," he said.

"Hello, gorgeous."

He laid one of those cheap real estate papers filled with grainy pictures of housing on my desk. "Check this out, man," he said. He flipped through three pages before finding the listing he wanted. "Right here, dude. Check this out. *Luxury two-bedroom.* Do you see the price?"

It was the first thing I saw. "$1200"

"Incredible, right?"

I had to recalibrate for a moment, because I realized, suddenly, that this would be a reality soon and that if I didn't want it, I would have to put my foot down now. But, when I thought about it, I realized I had no real reservations. The idea excited me. I wanted to move in with Ollie. The idea of new surroundings jolted me out of the depression of another work day. "That's fucking amazing," I said, amping my enthusiasm to match his.

"I'm going to pull the trigger. You're on month-to-month, right?"

"Yeah," I said.

"Good, me too." He sat down across from me, taking the paper with him. "This is gonna be great," he said, half to himself.

And what could I say? I believed him.

3

AT WORK, our misery took a backseat to planning our move-in. For once, we were no longer outsiders. Coworkers began to talk to us, because suddenly, we were talking about something less grotesque than our own glorious demise.

"Moving on up, eh, boys?"

"Don't go to the Eastside, for your own good. My favorite bike got stripped for parts by tweakers in broad daylight."

"Palatial Living—my cousin has an apartment there. Nice place."

And when we weren't nodding and saying, "Ah, yeah, gotcha," to the continued commentary, we were figuring how our two lives would end up fitting together.

"Are we keeping your couch?"

"No, I like yours better."

"How big is your TV?"

"60 inch."

"Fuck, okay. Let's go with that."

Through all of our combined worldly possessions, we created an optimized amalgam of our intertwining lives. We were the very best of two people who hated everything.

On the way to the apartment, for the first time, Ollie drove and we played our favorite game.

I started. "So, if you were going to do it, where would you start?"

"What do you mean? Like, would I plan it?"

"Sure. Let's say, you're at step one—you've decided you want to commit an atrocity. What do you do next?"

He thought on this for a minute, turning the wheel. "I think I'd decide what day of the week I want to do it—that's Monday, by the way."

"That's obvious. Everyone hates Mondays. I'd go for Friday though, for maximum trauma. Everyone wants to be killed on a Monday, but no one wants to die on a Friday."

He slapped the steering wheel. "I knew I kept you around for a reason. So, yeah, let's say Friday. But more important than day of the week is time of day. I'm thinking it'd be better to do it early in the day, as it'll create this sort of meta-narrative of all the world's drones empathizing with the poor bastards who got blown apart at their shitty jobs on a Friday."

"And not to forget the media coverage."

"That's true too. There's a lot of benefits to creating a tragedy during working hours."

"It primes everyone for a Long Hard Talk on Gun Violence."

"Or Mental Health."

"Or both, really."

"And they have all weekend to talk about it, to really stew in it. Marinade themselves in the crying mothers breathlessly telling their shit-tier memories of their sad sack kid who got his spine shattered by a stray bullet."

"Or, the manfully crying father who gruffly says that 'the time for healing has begun.'"

"Oh yeah, it takes a village, man. It takes a fucking village. As soon as the shit hits the fan, we're all signed up for the school play. So, let's talk real life—let's say that on a boring, un-cinematic day like Tuesday, someone snaps and opens fire on us in the office. Who are you when the camera rolls?"

He turned to me when he asked me this, staring, for maybe just a little too long. I was about to tell him to keep his eyes on the road, but instead I made a joke. "Corpse #1."

Ollie's eyes met the road again. He laughed. "I'm right there with you. Sign me up for Corpse #2. But that's the thing of it right—of all the people immediately involved in one of these Big American Tragedies, your best shot at having a piece of the action is being a dead guy. It's a very modest role, just about anyone can play it. So, if on this hypothetical Tuesday, anything were to go down, our role would likely only be seen on the news as: 11 Dead At Dead-End Job."

"And just like that—our lives reduced to that most unattractive of fractions: 2/11."

Ollie sighed. He put the car in park. "This is the joint. Let's try to be normal for our new landlord."

"No death-talking?"

"None today. Save it for when the contract is signed."

We went inside and the nice woman in business-casual clothes asked us our names and took notes on our income level and available deposit. Of course, Ollie had all this covered. Together, we were strong. There was no struggle coming up with a deposit, our combined incomes were more than enough to handle this mid-range luxury apartment.

In the blink of an eye—starting that day, when we walked the grounds, nodding and hmm-ing to the pretty woman who showed us everything with a magician's flourish, and ending a month later, where we were packed up, cramming our shit into a U-Haul that went from my apartment then to Ollie's and then to our new place—in a blink of an eye, our lives were no longer separate.

***

And everything was fine. No, really.

We were great. In all the ways you could imagine two male friends being great. We didn't argue about dumb shit, we didn't spend too much time with each other and suddenly become mortal enemies. We both innately knew that to preserve our friendship, we needed to stay the fuck away from each other, at least a little bit. So, when we got out of work and got back home (we carpooled now, of course), we generally went to our own bedrooms to unwind. We still planned our hang-outs, even if we lived in the same house.

He'd text me: "Hey, wanna watch something later?"

Then, me, from my room: "Sure!" but I'd yell it through the wall.

And that's how shit was for us. It was easy. We gave each other space. The only time I thought that there might be a problem was the whole incident with the girls.

4

WHILE WE CONSTANTLY talked about sex, masturbation, and dating, we never really made good on any of it. Eventually, it was Ollie who broached the subject and its real-world implications.

"So," he started, feet up on the coffee table, body melting into the sofa. "What are we going to do if we bring girls over?"

I hadn't thought about it much. It didn't seem like a real question. "Historically, I've fucked in my own bed. But, if you're offering . . . "

"No, I mean, like, are we a tag-team?"

I cocked an eyebrow. "Are you trying to get me to double-team someone?"

"No, well maybe. I'm thinking more like, are we wing-manning for each other? Like, if I brought a chick over, are you disappearing or are you out here entertaining her friend."

"Assuming she's brought a friend."

"Right."

I thought about it for a moment, because honestly, the whole idea of bringing over gaggles of women to divide and conquer seemed pretty at-odds with my current sexual strategy which involved meekly befriending women in my life until they decided to make a mistake. "Yeah, I guess so. Sure."

Ollie nodded. "Okay, good. I want to try it. I've never had a wing-man."

"Where are you getting these women?"

Ollie shrugged. "I don't know, I don't know. But they're out there."

In the next week, Ollie started wearing cologne. He also was away from his desk more. I didn't mind so much—I knew he was performing for me.

I heard from two desks over.

"Hey," he said, stretching it out for a beat too long. "Bri, what's happening?"

"Nothing much."

"Did you think about that thing? Friday night? Party?"

Bri's voice went bright and sharp. "Oh yeah! I think Kayla's going too, she's my ride. Do we need to bring anything?"

"Never," he said. "Both of you are more than enough."

And then he'd move on, with similarly corny, off-putting lines, and more people would mark their calendars. Ollie never told me we were having a party, I inferred it from his interactions, the silent planning he did on the couch and at work. He needed something, anything, to take his mind off the misery of his existence. And so did I. Now that the move-in was done and life had become almost too normal to handle, the party was the logical next step in transforming our lives into endless sublimation rituals.

Friday night came, and I was surprised to see how many people arrived. Ollie was smart, he'd invited enough men so that it didn't seem like we were slavering animals on the prowl for female meat. The ratio was favorable, but not suspicious.

I hugged Kayla when she entered. We were friendly, but not friends. "Nice to see you," I said. "Looking good, what is that? Cashmere?"

"Target clearance, actually, but thank you for noticing."

"Well, well, well—straight from Paris, I see."

Ollie touched my back in a clandestine manner, to hint at approval. I don't think he'd ever seen me talk to the opposite sex before.

"So, you two are roomies now?"

"More than that," he said, hugging me from behind.

I played along, nestling my head into his. "Much more."

"Aw, they're so cute," said Bri. "Adorable."

Ollie released me. "But serious now—beer, cider, Coke?"

"Powder or cola?"

He winked mysteriously. "Whatever the lady prefers."

"Cider would be lovely. And a shot," said Bri.

"Beer for me," added Kayla.

Ollie left me to talk to them while others filtered in. Kayla's husband had just decided to end their marriage a month ago and apparently this night out was fortuitously timed, as it was her first outing that hadn't revolved around her divorce. I nodded along and mugged empathetically. Kayla was fairly basic, if I was being honest. And I didn't know much about her beyond what I saw. But I also had the feeling that Ollie brought her for me, like he was feeding me or something, as a favor, so I felt it was my duty to talk to her and make a good show of it, whether I felt sparks flying or not.

"Yeah, so it's just been a tough month—"

Rich and Erik clapped their hands as they entered. My head pivoted from whatever boring shit Kayla was saying. "We brought some liquor, if anyone likes liquor . . . " They were obviously drunk.

"Excuse me," I said, thankful for the intrusion.

"My guys! What is up?"

Ollie yelled from across the apartment. "The gentlemen have arrived!"

Rich and Erik were not close to us, but they weren't enemies. They were sort of a bizarro version of Ollie and me, except where we filled the space of dark-humored jokesters, they were more like two aging frat bros. Both were around forty. One was divorced, although I couldn't for the life of me remember who. Rich was taller, with graying hair and a mouth that seemed to perpetually be on the verge of smiling.

Erik was smaller, but not by too much—he was the one who worked out almost religiously, regularly showing videos of his squats.

"The boys here brought the good stuff!" said Ollie, pouring Glenlivet into a plastic cup. "To Friday night, may Monday never come!"

A chorus of cheers. And then more people came, and then some left, and some more came, and so on and so forth. People mingled and drank and pizza came and then pizza went and bottles were empty and eventually, the party dwindled naturally. At a little past two, it was only Ollie, me, Bri, Kayla, and a guy named Karl from the office who was now realizing he was the odd man out and graciously said his goodbyes.

Ollie was shitfaced. I was, too, but not as bad as Ollie. He had sunk into the couch and somehow, Bri had snuggled up next to him. She was stoned out of her mind though, so I didn't see any real sexuality at play there. I just assumed she thought his slow breathing was somehow akin to listening to a seashell and hearing the ocean. Kayla, meanwhile, was moving her head in a measured, six-point motion, explaining quickly that her vertigo was acting up and the motions helped to make the room stop spinning. I was on the recliner, nursing a beer, feeling pleasant and drunk but also like the night had run its course and it was time to order the women a cab.

But before I could find an elegant way to ask them to leave, Ollie opened his eyes.

"So, it's just us," he said, and I could see that his eyes were glazed over, with drooping lids. His words were just so slightly slurred. "Just us. Just the four of us." He moved his arm and Bri blinked her eyes rapidly as if she had just come out of a trance. "So . . . ladies. I have a question for you."

I sat forward, interested.

"And it's not the question you think it is, alright? I couldn't fuck either of you if I wanted to. Whiskey dick runs in my family, it's a terrible shame. I won't speak for my comrade here, though, so leave your options open."

I smiled in a way that I hoped communicated *please, come on, don't take this guy seriously.*

Bri looked at him expectantly, but not annoyed. Kayla discontinued her head motions, but kept her eyes closed. She breathed deep.

"So, here's the question: you wake up one morning and you know for a fucking fact that nothing is ever going to be better than it is that day. You wake up and you have $113 in your bank account. You go to work at a job you hate. Your mind melts there because there's just nothing that can make you whole. So, one day, you wake up—I know, I know, I said that already, stay with me—you wake up and you find a gun. But it's not a regular gun. It's a Magic Gun. And this gun, it kills people in a way that obliterates them entirely. You try it on your annoying neighbor and find it very entertaining. It makes his whole body shake and goo starts pouring out of his eyes, and then he falls to the ground and it's over in an instant. Bam! The dude disappears. It's a sexy gun too, this Magic Gun. You look good with it, you check yourself out in the mirror and say shit like, 'Damn, I look *good.*' You feel tough, strong with the Magic Gun. Maybe you buy some fatigues because you think it completes your look. In some ways, this Magic Gun changes you entirely, makes you into a you that you kinda-sorta enjoy being. I should, real quick, mention my favorite part about this Magic Gun—it removes consequences from the act of killing. That's why it's Magic. So, you have your gun and you use it on the side, all sly-like. But that becomes a little boring, right? Way too boring. You have the greatest thing you've ever seen at your disposal, a consequence-free weapon of mass destruction, and you still have to go to work every day. So, my question to you is, how many days can you go before killing everyone you meet?"

A laugh roared out from my gut, but I was the only one laughing. The door slammed shut before he even finished the question. Kayla and Bri were outside on their phones and I could hear them urgently calling for a cab. We looked at each other with a hint of knowing, of mirth.

Ollie closed his eyes and started to drift off again. "It's good to be alone," he murmured.

"Yeah," I said. "I guess the party was a success." But I was just talking to myself.

5

I KNOCKED ON Ollie's door, because we were running behind. I had his coffee out on the table, poured into his thermos, and I was shaking my keys, saying, "C'mon, man. We gotta go. We're gonna be late."

I listened. Nothing.

"Dude, c'mon. We gotta go."

This time I heard a rustling. Blankets moving, a body tangled in sheets. A head turning on a pillow. Eventually: "I'm not feeling well," came the muffled voice. "Can you tell them I'm sick?"

This was the first time Ollie had called out since we moved in together. "Okay," I said slowly. "Sure. Yeah, of course." I didn't like it, but I did my best to be supportive. "Anything you want me to pick up for you tonight? Some medicine or something?"

"Nah," he said. "I just need rest."

"Well, okay. Sure, no problem. I'll let them know."

The day at work was a drag. A part of me craved some lasting controversy from Ollie's outburst, but it seems as though everyone moved on fairly quickly. There'd been no fallout from the party. Kayla and Bri gave me the same curt nods they always did, and sometimes, in passing, there was a hint of something warmer—a quick question, a greeting. If they were mad about the other night, there was no hint of it. I found the whole thing hilarious, because I found Ollie hilarious in pretty much everything he did. But, I was stuck between my admiration for him and my desire to fly under the radar.

I put numbers into a spreadsheet and kept darting my eyes to the door, imagining an explosion blowing them off their hinges, or neon green gas seeping in through the cracks. I decided all of that would be just fine. Every stapler click was the sweet sound of a round being chambered and I closed my eyes and waited for it to paint my brains onto the wall.

When I got home, Ollie was still in his room. "Missed ya today, buddy."

"How'd it go?"

"No one's mad at you, if that's what you're saying." I felt stupid talking to him through a closed door. "You feeling any better?"

"A little," he said. "But I need a little more rest. Just gonna go back to sleep for the rest of the night, if that's alright."

I checked my phone. It was 5:15 PM. "Alright, man. Whatever you need."

Not having Ollie to discuss the day with made me feel all the more isolated, so I turned on the television and grabbed a beer to complete my after-work ritual alone.

And it was fine, I guess.

Except, I couldn't quite shake the feeling that Ollie wasn't asleep at all.

Every once in a while, my ears would perk up. *Was that movement?* I thought, as humans, some of our old predator brains remained. I liked to think that we were still not any better than the animals we kept as pets, that somewhere deep inside of us was primitive instinct. And I liked to think that one of those instincts was the ability to sense movement. Like, picture this: say you were in a jungle or something and everything was dead silent. And then, all of a sudden, you froze. Was something watching you? You couldn't see anything, but you suddenly felt like something was, right?

How the fuck would we know that a puma was looking at us?

Well, I don't know, maybe we wouldn't. But, I do know that I kept the remote right by my side the entire night, finger on the mute button, because I had a feeling that Ollie was not only awake, but busy.

***

Ollie kept calling out, and I kept having to go to work alone, which made me increasingly upset. At work, I tried reaching out to other co-workers, but that only highlighted my isolation.

"How are you doing?"

"Good."

"You?"

"Fine."

"What happened to Ollie?"

"Sick."

"Ah, gotcha," they'd say. "Hope he feels better."

And that'd be the only conversation I'd have.

So, besides being bored and depressed and each shift feeling like it had doubled in length, there was also the issue of me never seeing Ollie at all, except in the briefest moments.

When I saw him on Wednesday, he was wearing a robe and he was in the kitchen and when he noticed I was in—he must not have heard me open and close the front door—he made like a spooked deer and ran back to his room.

"You doing okay?"

"Yeah, fine, man."

"Haven't seen you in a while. You wanna have a beer or something?"

"No, no. I should get back to bed."

And then he was gone, and I was left peeling the sweaty label off a beer bottle.

Three days later I saw him again and sometimes I wonder what would've happened if he'd just stayed in his room, forever. Surely, everything would've been better.

6

TO MY SURPRISE, Ollie was up before me. As I wiped the gunk from my eyes, I realized he was also in my room. We didn't have a lot of written rules as roommates, but if we were going to have one: entering the other's room without permission was a serious no-go.

But I hadn't seen him in so long and he was vibrant and wide awake and I was too tired to care.

"Ollie, you're alive."

He waved a hand at me. "Please, I can never die." He did a little dance and said, "C'mon, man. Get up. I got a surprise for you."

I rubbed my eyes. "Jesus, man. I could've used a bit more sleep."

"You'll sleep when you're dead. I did something nice for you, man, get the fuck up. We're gonna have a wild day. *Wild.* Living room, now."

So, I got up. Stumbling from sleepiness, I managed to throw myself onto the couch and sit up. I noticed Ollie was just wearing shorts and a T-shirt. "Feeling better?" I asked.

"Great, man. Thanks for asking." He stood in front of me, like he was about to give a speech.

"You going to work today?"

"Nope."

"Oh," I said, crestfallen.

He smiled, though. "But neither are you. I called in for you."

"Excuse me?"

"God, don't pretend you don't have sick pay. You never call out."

"Well, well . . . yeah. Okay." I shook my head. I had to get used to the idea. Despite hating my job maybe more than anything in the world, societal pressure kept me locked into the idea of being 'stable,' whatever that meant. I remembered working with my dad for a little at his boring office job, hearing the hatred he had in his voice, the snide comments from co-workers about so-and-so having brown bag flu. The thought of people talking about me behind my back, *hating* me, filled me with a potent sense of dread.

"They believed me, don't worry. I do a really good impression of that droney, bored sounding voice you do on the phone, like you're trying to be the vocal epitome of drying paint."

"Do I really—?"

"Don't worry about that. I got something to tell you. It's big. Something I've been working on."

"You've been working?"

"For years."

I settled into my chair. "Okay," I said. "I'm listening."

He stood in front of me. "First off, though, let me just congratulate you on your day-off. Nothing better than a do-nothing Thursday, am I right? I feel bad that you always go to work when you can put your PTO to use and maybe just relax for a minute. It's a good feeling, dude. Anyways, yeah. I've been working."

"So. Let me start with a question: have you ever had one of those days that felt just a little more real than another?"

"The thought never really occurred to me."

"Sure, and the thought never occurred to me until I thought about it, so you are forgiven, young padawan. Of course you don't know shit about that. It's not a part of your reality, yet. This idea, I mean, the idea that some days are more real than others."

"What does that even mean?"

"That's a great question. And it's one I'll do my best to answer, but I have to warn you, the details, out of necessity, will be fuzzy, indistinct, and subjective. It might frustrate you to a degree, because really, it takes mostly intuition to decide how real a day is. Over the last nine months, I've been cataloging the days that I thought weren't very real. So, like, I have a spreadsheet, man. Huge-ass Excel spreadsheet where every day is accounted for in the last nine months with a list of keywords."

I was starting to feel scared. "You sound crazy, dude. Do you want to go somewhere? I could drive you."

He held up a hand. "Believe me, dude. I'm not crazy." He lowered himself slightly, as if he were trying to appear less threatening. "I've already gotten myself checked out a couple times. I actually have the outpatient work right here. They say I have problems with depression and intrusive thoughts, but no hallucinations. I'm sane. Pretty normal they said. You can see the papers if you want."

"I might take you up on that," I said, eyeing my friend carefully.

Ollie took a deep breath. "You know what? You're right. Be right back." He left the room and came back with a tan folder. "You'll notice I've been three times in the last nine months, last time was last week, on the first day I called out of work. It was sort of prep for me telling you this. I mean, I get it, you know? This shit sounds crazy and I knew the first thing that would come up if I talked to you about it would be: 'dude, you sound crazy.'"

I flipped through the files quickly, probably more quickly than I should have. It was embarrassing doing this, even if Ollie was my best friend, it felt like a breach of trust. But, it was as he said: depression, depression and anxiety once, and depression and intrusive thoughts.

"You're not hallucinating," I said, finally. "According to these esteemed professionals." I tried to sound funny about it. "Lay it on me, keep going."

"I'm calling it a Tidal Reality. Because really, reality isn't just a static force. It's not just there and then it keeps going, it's more like a tide that goes in and out. Reality has an ebb and flow to it."

I considered this, trying to understand what he was saying. I held up three fingers. "How many fingers am I holding up?"

"Twelve," he said, deadpan. "Today is real, if you're wondering. Totally, 100% real. I go through my checklist every day to see what's going on."

"So, on the days that are unreal, is that when you call out?"

"Yes! Exactly! I knew you'd get it."

"Um, why? I don't understand."

"Because they don't matter. There's no real consequences to those days. They just happen and then vanish from our collective memory. I bet you couldn't remember anything that happened on an unreal day. You know how days at work slip together, right? How everything just kinda becomes this sludge? Well, yeah, that's the Tidal Reality at work."

"It's not that doing the same thing every day makes it hard to distinguish specific days?"

"No, that's what makes it hard to distinguish the Tidal Reality. Because both are happening at once. With both of those things happening—you almost have no chance at figuring it out. It was basically a miracle that I did."

"And how did you decide this was a thing?" I felt like going along for the ride. Ollie had a way about him where, even when he was talking absolute bullshit, he still managed to have me hanging on his every word.

"By total chance, man. Just ridiculous, stupid chance. I started to notice things when I broke my routine during monotonous days. Like, you might not know this about me, but I'm a pretty keen observer of human nature. That sounds dumb, I know, but seriously. I remember stuff about people. There was one day I came in a little late and it was as if everything went off its rocker. You've had days like that, right? Where you miss one key step of your routine and suddenly everything feels like it's going to topple over? Well, that's what happened to me. I sat down across from you and you looked up at me and usually you say, 'Sup, dude,' but that day you said, 'Morning, Ollie.' Now, that's not a big deal, right? Sometimes we change up our greetings and at the time it didn't do much for me, it just made me think: 'huh, sounded a little off.' But then afterwards, I began noticing all these other things. Kayla almost always curls her hair before work, but that day her hair was straight. The break room didn't have any decaf made, and when I asked Roger about it, because he has hypertension, he just shrugged and said, 'eh, I can live a little.' I started keeping a journal of all of these deviations, no matter how small. Do you see?"

"No, not at all. Are you saying we're not real? Are you saying there's some grand conspiracy against you and we're all changing our routines slightly to make you crazy? Because honestly, it might be working."

He chuckled, but it was a pained chuckle. He knew he was losing me. "No, not at all. Not at all, man. You're not doing anything I wouldn't do in your situation, or rather, have done in your situation. Let me try to explain this, because it's weird. Birds are able to fly north and south because of some sort of magnetic switch in their brain. It's like instinct, right? Think about that. How does that shit even work? Well, I think, and I know not everyone is like this, but if you went to a strange place, would you have a sense of where north was?"

I thought about it. As a kid, I was always frustrated when I gave cardinal directions to my little sister and she often went walking in the opposite way. "Yeah," I said, pointing.

"Thank God," he said, rubbing his forehead. Apparently, this was a key win for him. "That's good. I would've totally lost you if you couldn't. It's called magnetoreception though, some people think it's a lost sense. So, I guess, think of that fleeting feeling you get when you just know where North is.

Now, it's not so hard to believe that that same sense, or maybe a similar one, can sense when your timeline has changed, and as a provision, or maybe a release, your brain just says: 'fuck it, man!' So, you try something different. Maybe that deep awareness that something is off lets you change up your muscle memory and allows you to say 'Morning, Ollie,' instead of 'Sup, dude.' Or maybe it lets you drink regularly caffeinated coffee because you know it won't matter tomorrow when the Tide rolls back. Or maybe you change your hairstyle. The point is, your body is telling you: the world you know isn't right, so stop living by its rules."

I thought about this for a minute and then sighed. "Ollie, man. This shit is fucking crazy."

He nodded. "I know, man. I really know. But also know this: the next unreal day is tomorrow, and I want you to be prepared for what's going to happen." He paused for a moment, swallowed. "That's a Friday, by the way."

7

BY THE TIME tomorrow came, I was tired and totally sleepless. I wasn't stupid, I knew the importance of Friday. I could read all the writing on the wall. Friday equaled something bad. It meant Ollie might be going too far, doing something too bad for even me to get on board with.

But also, as I lay awake in bed all night, it hit me that it meant every conversation he and I had would be put under a microscope, and somehow, I too would be made to be an enabler, an accomplice, whether I ever pulled a trigger or not.

My day off was spent talking back and forth with Ollie who seemed at ease with the idea of doing something drastic to prove his point, although he wouldn't say what it was. I thought about calling the police. But, it was easier said than done. Ollie was my friend, and he hadn't actually done anything yet. As far as I knew, he didn't own a single weapon. He'd never hurt anyone before. All he had was a dumbass theory. But there was another reason that kept me from calling anyone for help—Ollie was remarkably calm and unstressed. He didn't seem particularly worried about what would happen tomorrow, only repeating that I should wait and see. And for some reason, although I was worried out of my mind about what that could mean, I didn't think he meant for anything awful to happen.

When I got out of bed, Ollie was already dressed and waiting for me. "Made you coffee," he said.

"Thanks."

"You okay, dude?"

"I didn't sleep much."

"Ah shit," he said. "Sorry, man." He took a sip of his coffee cup. "I know this shit can be pretty overwhelming. Don't worry though. It'll be good. Nothing that happens today will be able to ripple past the Tidal Reality."

I winced. I hated hearing him say it, as if it were real. It wasn't real. It was stupid. I ground my teeth. "Dude," I said. "Please don't do anything stupid. Seriously. Please."

He shook his head, slapped me on the shoulder. "C'mon, man. Just relax, please. Remember that tomorrow, everything will be reset. Like *Groundhog's Day*, sorta."

On the way to work, he played the radio loud and sang nonsense words to songs he'd never heard. He was trying to make me laugh, get me to loosen up a bit. When we pulled into the parking lot, my hands were shaking, and he gave me one last pep talk.

"Alright. So, you have a mission today. I need you to be observant of all the little things. I'm not doing anything today until I know for sure the Tidal Reality is at its peak, okay?"

"What am I noticing?"

"Anything, small things. Stuff that seems different than usual. That's all. Can you do that for me? Treat it like a game, alright? We're gonna try to rack up some high scores today."

The wording made me freak, internally. But I had to remind myself that nothing bad was happening yet. There was no sign that our talks about death and disaster were going to rear their smiling faces and lick their slavering jaws. Nothing had happened.

When we went inside, Ollie greeted reception with a "Holla, girl." And when we passed, he said, "Did you see that?"

I looked back at him with a dumb stare.

"She didn't even notice. That's a weird thing not to notice."

My heart was pumping in my chest. "I don't think it was anything, dude. She was reading something. She was busy. She didn't hear you." My whispers were becoming harsh.

"Nah, she heard me alright," he said. "Of course she did. But don't worry, we'll have more to investigate."

When we got to our desk, I began to work in earnest. Unfortunately, that was more challenging than it sounded. Looking across the desk, Ollie was sitting back, drinking coffee from his thermos. I had half a mind to tell him to get to work, but I stopped because I realized that it would be out of character. It made me wonder why I wanted to work in the first place. Why did I care if Ollie worked? I was nervous, of course. Scared.

But, also—thrilled. I decided to let go.

I smiled to myself and pushed my keyboard away. I suddenly got it. That bastard. "Okay," I said. "You win. I'm playing."

Ollie grinned. "Yes! I knew you'd get into it."

I chuckled to myself, shaking my head. This was a game. He told me straight away that it was a game. How could I be so stupid? There was no Tidal Reality. There was nothing here but Ollie trying to make a shitty situation better. We were at work. We hated being at work. So, he invented a game. I wanted to clap for him, because it was genius. I sat there for a moment, admiring my friend, admiring how he turned people watching into our new escapism.

"So, what have you seen so far?" I asked.

He pulled up something from underneath the table. "I've been keeping notes," he said, showing his notepad. He wasn't lying, it was full. He was taking this really seriously, I realized, with a bit of jabbing weakness. He'd been writing nonstop for his first hour of work, as if he were trying to make a quota. He continued, "Olivia is eating at her desk. Carl, the dumbass, is talking to Raj by the watercooler—and he hates Raj—told me himself. I think the clocks are like a quarter second slow today. I'm not sure, every time I count the seconds out, I'm pretty sure it takes an extra second for it to move four seconds on the clock. It's usually right on, you know? I count it every day. It's one of those small things. Anyways. Kayla is using her left hand to write today. Did you know she's ambidextrous? I actually noticed that at the party, we talked about it for a minute while you were mingling. She favors her right hand for most everything though, she says, even though she can do it all with both. But yeah, today she's using her left. Look at her."

I did. Just as Ollie said, she was writing with her left hand. I wasn't sure if I should be annoyed at this or excited. It was a game. "Okay," I said, trying to remain calm, fun, and carefree. *We're having fun*, I reminded myself. "So, I did notice one thing today."

Ollie looked up from his list. "Oh, yeah?"

I swallowed. It wasn't anything big. Nothing big at all. But I'd noticed it, for sure. I felt stupid noticing it at all. "The numbers," I said, pointing to my computer screen. "They're all sequential."

"What?"

"See for yourself. One, two, three, four, five, and so on and so forth."

His eyes widened. "That's insane." He leaned back in his chair. "You fucking genius."

"Not bad for a beginner," I said, but there was a tremor in my voice.

"Why would they be sequential, that doesn't make any sense?" He was talking to himself now. "You can do that shit with any simple function, that's Excel 101. They don't need us to generate—well, fuck, it's just counting, really." He took a deep breath and stared me deep in the eye. "You done good, kid. Real fucking good."

"Thanks, man. But it's just a game, right?"

Ollie reached for something under his desk. "Hey, man, do me a favor—stay cool until tomorrow, alright?"

"What does that mean?"

SOFT TARGETS

It took me a second to see what he had pulled out. "Just trust the plan."

"What does that—oh shit, is that a fucking *gun*?"

He placed the barrel to his temple.

"You'll see," he said, and then pulled the trigger.

8

OLLIE'S HEAD EXPLODED. At least that was what it looked like at first. Before he died, he had that same *wish me luck* look he always had before he was about to do something daring, cavalier, stupid—like the face of an Old Hollywood star about to pull one over on the audience one final time.

Except now, his face was cratered in on the side, his neck was limp, and I was covered in a fine mist of his blood. Chunks of bone were on his keyboard. Thick slugs of flesh and brain matter crawled from the gaping wound.

And everyone was screaming. Everyone. Me, I was screaming. I was crying.

I didn't know what to do. I stood up, I guess, I rushed over to him, I guess. And then people were pulling me away.

"Ollie!" I shouted.

And they said, "No, no, don't touch him. Stand back." But instead of letting me stand back they pulled me back.

The gun had fallen to the office carpet and we all just let it lay there. I tried looking at it, just so I didn't have to look at Ollie.

Someone called 911. Someone told us to evacuate now, to not touch anything. I was pushed out by empathetic hands. It was as if I were floating at sea. Gentle waves took me away, and I had no idea what was happening. I was utterly without agency and in a blink of an eye, I was out in the parking lot. People, co-workers, touched my shoulders in stunned silence. When the police arrived, people whispered questions to me: "Are you alright? Are you hurt? What happened?"

And I couldn't say anything. I was too sad, too scared. Too overwhelmed in the moment. Somebody hugged me and I was falling into their arms, burying my face into their shoulder, and I was sobbing violently, like a maniac. When I could finally speak, they took my story down as quickly and quietly as they could, away from the others. They turned me around when the body came out on a stretcher. The officer taking my story told me, "Hey, no one will blame you if you need to see someone."

And like a child, I sniffled and nodded and clumsily stuffed the card for a therapist into my wallet.

"It's really no big deal, especially for something like this. He was your roommate, you said?"

"Yeah," I said, numb.

The cop whistled. "Tough break, man. I'm sorry for your loss."

I didn't feel like I had any real agency. I was pushed between crowds, hugged back and forth, spoken to like a child. Finally, it came to an end as the fervor lost its luster.

"Everyone, take the rest of the day off," said Kev. I was still in a daze, walking into people, crying my eyes out. And just as the words were said, everyone got into their cars and left and I was left sitting in my car, where Ollie and I drove together that morning, where I was annoyed and scared and I had every right to be. I felt the guilt burning a hole in my stomach. I could've done something. I could've called someone. The police or someone better, maybe. A crisis counselor, if those actually existed. I didn't feel right about any of it, I knew something was wrong, and I did nothing. I did absolutely nothing. And in the end, it was my fault. It was my fault that Ollie's brains were drying on his desk.

I drove home through wet eyes, barely able to see the road. When I got to the apartment, I collapsed on the couch to absolute emptiness. There were no sounds coming from his room. The instinct, that sixth sense, of knowing someone was around, had vanished. I was fucking alone and Ollie was gone.

I fell asleep on the couch, a deep, horrible sleep where I dreamt of nothing. The whole time, I could taste the snot in the back of my throat. It was an awful blackness. Shitty, shitty blackness. I'd jolt awake every so often, when a car parked outside or the refrigerator hummed or the clock on the wall, Ollie's clock, ticked.

For a moment of wakefulness, I counted those ticks. And I tried to remember what Ollie said about them earlier today. I tried to remember everything he said on his last day to make sense of it all, but I was too tired. I was dead tired. Eventually, I got up off the couch and shambled zombie-like to my bed. The sleep continued, but this time with dreams. Vivid dreams where I was looking at Ollie and I had the gun and I was putting it to my own head and I was pulling the trigger and the explosion blew my eardrums out and my neck snapped my head to the side as the bullet entered and then everything went black, again and again and again.

And then, suddenly, I woke up.

I blinked.

I wiped my eyes.

I snuffled my nose and took in a lungful of snot and coughed.

That thing, the thing at the back of your head that told you you were being watched—that was an air-raid siren right now. It was screaming in my ear: *you're not alone, you're not alone!*

It was morning, I realized, or almost morning anyways. The light from my window was gray and the sky was indigo, it must've been only minutes before sunrise.

Footsteps, a creak.

I blinked again.

I realized my door was ajar.

A shape.

"It worked, didn't it?"

My jaw dropped. I scrambled out of bed as my eyes adjusted further.

"Ollie?" I asked.

And the voice, the shape, replied: "He lives."

9

AT FIRST, I thought I was dreaming, which is a dumb thing to think, but I wasn't sure which part was the dream. Did Ollie kill himself in my nightmare? Did Ollie resurrect as an apparition of my hope?

"I'm real," he said, sounding haggard. It was as if he heard my thoughts. "Real as shit, dude."

I moved toward him and then suddenly recoiled. He noticed. He laughed.

"Dude, c'mon. It's me. Just like what I said would happen. It didn't count."

"What are you talking about?"

And I realized suddenly that I couldn't remember why I was crying. It was gone, like how a dream just starts to evaporate after you wake up. I remembered some of it, instances, I still had the heaviness in my heart, but for some reason, I couldn't articulate what had happened. And this scared me.

"You don't remember," he said.

"No, no—I remember," I said. But I was lying to myself.

"What do you remember? We'll need to start keeping dream journals, I think. That can be a part of the process."

"Something—something—something happened at work, right?"

"Yeah."

"Everyone was sad, upset. Was there a shooting?"

"Yeah, sort of."

He gave me the details, quickly, nervously, as if he were embarrassed by them. It all sounded so strange and otherworldly to me. "You killed yourself." Saying it out loud brought a faint memory, of my friend lifting the gun, the sharp crack of a sound that hurt my ears. "I—I was there."

"Yeah, you were. That's good. Jeez, this is going to sound stupid, but I have a splitting headache."

I didn't laugh. "You killed yourself," I said again. "You never told me that you had any, you know, *issues*."

He waved a hand. "I did, actually. Just the day before I did it. We all have issues, dude. But please, don't get all sentimental on me. I just did it to test the Tidal Reality. It worked, right? I died and then reality was reset, right?"

"I'd totally forgotten about all of that—Jesus." I went back to my bed and sat down in the early morning light. "I can't believe any of this."

Ollie came to sit beside me and put a hand on my back. I almost recoiled from the touch—faint memories of being moved about like a doll, something from a dream, remained within me. "I didn't really think this through, man, and I'm sorry for that. I shouldn't have made you watch me blow my brains out. That'd be pretty rough to watch, I bet. I'm glad I didn't have to see it, you know? But, I also want you to know that everything from this point on can be a lot of fun, if we make it. That's why I'm doing any of this. Because it's fun."

"Killing yourself is fun?"

"No, no, no. Oh, ye of little imagination. If you found out that there were days you could do anything, that nothing mattered, what would you do?"

I had to admit, I'd never thought of it that way. I understood Ollie's jabber, but not what it *meant*. He was looking for a way out. A way to make life interesting, worth living.

"So, this is it," he said. "It's real. What do we do?" And I realized he was really asking me. It was just, I had no idea what to say. What could I possibly say now?

"Did it hurt?"

"Yeah," he said. "But just for a second. Barely anything, really. It was like one millisecond of really sharp pain and then total oblivion, like a deep sleep—but without, you know, consciousness. It's hard to describe the lack of consciousness. It wasn't like I was asleep, it was like I was deleted."

"How did you come back?"

"I just woke up in bed. Probably where I would've been the day before if nothing had happened."

"Huh."

"Yeah. Weird shit."

"Everyone—well, I can't remember now—but I have these feelings, you know—like everyone was probably pretty torn up. Do you think work is canceled?"

"It's Saturday, dude. And no. They won't remember it. This isn't my first stunt."

"You've done this before."

"Nothing like this, but other things. Outbursts, running and screaming. Took a shit in the coffee pot once."

"No shit?"

"Yep."

"What'd I do?"

"You were dying, man. Like, crying tears."

"Jesus, I bet. What'd Kev do?"

"Straight up vomited. Just hunched over, grabbed his knees and threw his lunch up on the floor. I think a couple other people started doing that too."

"That happened?"

"Swear to God."

"Jesus," I said. "I can't remember it, not even a little."

"The next day was back to normal, everything was wiped, except for me. I wrote everything down after to be sure I remembered."

We just stood like that for a while, and then eventually we moved to the living room. It was only seven in the morning and Ollie already had a couple beers cracked open.

I didn't refuse. We drank and talked about what this meant and I kept trying to weasel my way out of this new reality that Ollie had presented to me. And then, whenever I did, he'd reel me back in with a new story, a new triumph from a past Tide. I'd be asking questions, wondering what I did in a different timeline. Talking about it was really learning about myself—peering into a different dimension to see me in all of my multi-faceted forms.

Did I believe him? I wasn't sure.

I didn't *not* believe him.

I was really just enthralled, at everything, the possibilities. The beer hit my lips and I was getting drunk as the rest of the world woke up. Ollie put an arm around me and everything was okay, almost. Even on the most perfect day, sitting at home, drinking with my best friend, I couldn't get rid of a dark feeling in my stomach, an echo of despair. I'd jump when I heard a loud noise. Out of nowhere, a creeping bit of mourning would come over me and I'd have to sniff and say aloud, "What was that?" while I wiped my eye. Ollie was cool about it though, he was always cool about it. "No problem," he'd say. "It's cool." And I'd forget it happened and just go on talking.

"When's the next Tide?" I asked, trying to sound casual about it.

"Next Wednesday."

"Do they happen every week?"

"Sometimes. Some more than others. Some weeks I've had three happen, sometimes it skips a week or two. It's hard to say. I try to predict them, but it's like the weather, you know? You don't always know it's gonna rain until your hair's wet."

"Right," I said. "Sure. Makes sense." And slowly, I realized, I wasn't lying.

10

WE DIDN'T DO anything bad on Wednesday.
Ollie was letting me get my feet wet, carefully. He had come to trust the Tidal Reality through many days of trial and error. He was confident in his abilities to live without consequences. He knew I would have to go through the same experience. I was scared shitless, of course, but I went along with it because of the lingering sorrow and triumphant awe from Ollie's Lazarus-like return.

On the first day, my first Wednesday, we tried a lot of things together. We talked long and loud about incest, mass killings, and dead children. This was as much as I was willing to commit to—I couldn't hurt myself or others. But I could talk, I could talk loud and be obnoxious. We forced horrible things to come out of our mouths and then, like so many other things that happened between me and Ollie, we made a game of it. We traversed taboo after taboo, louder and louder, my heart machine-gunning in my chest.

Those around us were shocked and disgusted, of course. Someone stood up and went to whisper and it was Kev— blond, effete Kev—who asked us to leave for the day. Ollie, being bolder, refused. I had a moment of panic where I thought that it was time to start begging to stay—a feeling that disgusted me. I was waiting for the hammer to drop and the realization to set in that I had just fucked up my life beyond repair. But Ollie just laughed. He chided Kev and encouraged me to chide him too, and as the blood pumped through my ears, I did my best to be Ollie's mimic.

"You . . . fucking suck," I said weakly.

Kev recoiled, his eyebrows raised. "Get out of here, both of you."

"Fuck you!"

"Yeah, fuck you!" I repeated.

Security escorted us out.

And the next morning, I woke up, the last day like a hazy dream, and went back to work. Nobody said anything to us. Nobody remembered our inglorious exit. Kev gave me the rundown of the day's work, with the same enthusiastic rigidity as always.

Full. Body. Chills.

Ollie elbowed me. "See?"

I'd gone along with it out of some desire to turn my steering wheel into oncoming traffic; the worst case scenario would be that I lost a job I already hated. But I didn't actually believe it was going to work.

But, there we were—another day; another excruciating day.

Then, the next Thursday, we started our day with bolder intentions still. The week in between had been duller than most, more full of dismissals and condescension. It was tedium with a chainsaw. Kev had heard that the numbers weren't as good as they should be, that a branch was out competing us, and that we had new quotas to make. For us, this meant overtime as we seldom put in even the most minimal of effort. Kev delivered this to us in the same dry, bootlicking way he always did.

He gathered us in a circle, all the lowly key-pushers, and said: "Alright, team. I appreciate all the hard work everyone has put in, but the numbers don't lie. We're slacking. We're falling behind and we need to, as a team, buck up and make this right." He went on to orate numerical benchmarks as if they were his personal prayer. "If that means overtime, we're gonna okay it. We don't care about overtime, we care about getting the work done. We don't want it to come to that though, we know you all have lives."

Ollie and I were sniggering in the back, mostly out of despair. We knew what he was getting at before he got there.

"From now on, we're going to be cracking down a lot more on non-essential, non-work activities. Watercooler talk, horseplay, you know. We need to get our numbers back on track."

I could've sworn he looked at us when he said it.

And for the next week, we made good on it, just as he said. Anytime Ollie and I would start talking, even quietly, Kev would pop in and say something professional and officious like, "Hey, guys—you haven't met your quotas for the day. Everyone else here would appreciate it if you focused on your work."

We'd nod and say, "Sure, alright, Kev. Whatever you say."

And let me tell you something here: after our first trip together through the Tide, a work week felt more like Hell than ever before. It was like having a taste of pure freedom, of knowing the heights that life could reach, only to be dragged back down and kicked in the guts. We were stuck typing numbers into a blinking cursor, all day, every day, without even the slightest hint of relief. Kev would walk around the desks and sometimes I'd imagine him with a riding crop. After work, Ollie and I would talk about how much we hated work, how much worse it'd become since the new quotas.

But it wouldn't be long, we knew. And when Thursday came, we were prepared. I was still stressed about the whole thing. I was constantly asking Ollie, "Well, what if it was all a dream?"

"It wasn't a dream, dude."

"That doesn't make it easier for me," I said. "I need proof."

"Well, go through with this today, and you'll have pretty good proof."

Shit like that always pissed me off about Ollie. My palms were sweating and I was freaking out because, well, we could go to jail, and he just told me to ignore everything inside of me screaming to stop and do it anyway.

That morning, we didn't go to work.

"C'mon, man. You're supposed to be having fun," he said. "Who knows how many of these days we have left?"

His wording made me feel sick to my stomach. "You think they can end?"

"Everything ends eventually, right? It might transform. It might just go away. I don't know if it's been here before and no one noticed or if it's been a recent thing. Is it just for me—or, for us, I guess now—or is it everyone? If I kept getting people involved, could we have this big-ass *Purge* society? And speaking of—does the Tide affect big cultural events? If a revolution happens on a day with a high Tide, does that mean it happened or did it not? Do they have to wait a day and do their overthrowing again? What about movies, though? If the reality isn't real the day a movie comes out, does none of the money count? If I rob someone, do I keep the money or does the money reset back to where it was? These are all big questions, my man—and I have zero answers to any of them. So, there's a lot we don't know."

But but but. "I'm just nervous, that's all."

Ollie shrugged. "Me too, man. Me too." He took a deep breath and lit up a joint and said, "Honestly, I've never done anything like this before."

"Not ever?"

"Nope. Always kept it pretty silly, the stuff I've done. Gross, sometimes. But mostly silly."

"We could bail on it, you know?"

Ollie moved his head back and forth, as if he were considering it. "We could," he said finally. "But just think about how that twat talks to us every day, man. Like we're fucking idiots. I mean, seriously, are you a fucking idiot? Don't you have a Master's or something?"

"Yeah. No, I get it. I can't fucking stand that guy."

"And it's not gonna do much, you know. It's not like I haven't done worse to myself." He mimed the gun to his temple and made a dramatic limping motion. My psyche jolted as he poked a residual memory.

"That's true."

"And he's gonna wake up like nothing happened."

"Yeah, hopefully."

"No—absolutely. We've already done the checklist, we're good."

He was right. I had started to get a feel for it. *Something* was off. *Something* didn't feel right. It was a siren in the back of my brain, repressed by years of training, maybe generations. We went for a walk and spotted birds flying in opposite directions. The usually busy street was totally empty. The corner store had a Closed sign on it. Ollie mused, "I wonder if he's a fellow traveler. No hate, shop dude. Enjoy your day off." Then, we turned on the television and watched the news. "This is my favorite," he said. "Seriously, it gets fucking weird."

And he was right, again.

The news anchor was sweating, his eyes pierced through the television screen. "There are things happening. There are *things* happening. I don't know what it is. I don't know what it is. Oh, Jesus. Won't you fucks just listen to me? Won't any of you listen to me? Something isn't fucking right. Count the stars, why don't you? They're going to shut me down, they're turning me off, think, think, think—"

"He always does this," said Ollie. "Old Jeffrey Masha—he knows about it too. Or, it happens for him too."

"Every Tide?"

"Oh yeah, he goes for it every time. They usually cut the channel before he gets too far, but the next day he still always has a job. Just like me."

I was shocked. I looked at Ollie. "Dude, way to bury the lede. Why didn't you show me this at first?"

He shook his head. "No, this isn't anything. Television gaffes are just that—gaffes. Jeff doesn't know what's going on, he just knows something is going on. He never explicitly states anything. It's like it's on the tip of his tongue. I think that's how it is for a lot of people, some people are closer to it than others."

"Jeffrey fucking Masha."

"Jeffrey fucking Masha," he agreed. After a moment, he looked at his phone. "Let's go crack some eggs, dude."

And really, it was because of Jeff Masha that we did what we did.

11

WE WAITED OUTSIDE for Kev. We were in Ollie's car, which we didn't usually take to work because it was an old junker. Ollie always seemed to wilt at the idea of people seeing him as lesser, so as soon as we moved in together, it became necessary to take my vehicle.

"How many times did they call you today?" he asked.

"Just once."

"Yeah, same."

"One call—no check up at all."

"It's fucking insulting," I said, trying to get my blood heated.

"It is!" Ollie agreed. "Here we are, obviously the two most depressed motherfuckers in the whole office, and all we do is talk about dying. Every fucking day—or used to, when Kev hadn't become a hall monitor yet—every fucking day we'd be talking about how we're just daydreaming of getting our brains blown out by some masked gunman, and now, the day we don't show up—a total no call, no show situation—they only call us once. They don't send anyone to check on us. Nothing happens."

"Because no one cares."

"No one fucking cares." He sighed. "Do you want a cigarette?"

Ollie had decided that when the Tide was high, he should start smoking.

"Sure," I said.

We lit up and waited. Sure enough, at 5:05, Kev was walking across the parking lot, typing something on his phone.

"Alright, this is it."

"Should we cover our faces?" I felt stupid when I asked it. "Never mind."

Ollie got out of the car first. "Kev, my man!" he called.

I followed him, keeping my hand behind my back. "What's happening, dude?" I tried to sound genial.

He looked up and swiveled his head from one to the other. "You two weren't at work today."

"Nope, afraid not," said Ollie.

"Okay," said Kev, looking more confused than anything. "Whatever." He looked down at his phone again to type something quickly. Something about his utter dismissal of us, as colleagues and people, enraged me. And if that weren't enough, when he turned, he said, off-handedly, "Not that it matters, made the quotas anyways."

Ollie nodded to me, but I was already making my strides.

You might be wondering how this happened. How one man can become so prone to violence after fretting about it constantly the entire morning. Well, the secret was in the Tidal Reality. Because the secret of the Tidal Reality was that it wasn't a secret—we all knew about it innately. We couldn't articulate it, but it was always there. Some days it urged us to strike a loved one, or wear a different tie, or drink regular instead of decaf. It was always there when it needed to be to heighten our impulsiveness.

So, when it came time to reveal the heavy wrench I had behind my back, it was no problem. On a normal day, Kev's comments would've wounded me. But when the Tide was high, they enraged me.

I swung the wrench at Kev's shocked face, knocking his open 'o' of a mouth closed upon impact. It landed with a wet crunching sound, and I was sure that I felt the vibrations of his teeth shattering down the handle and into my hand.

Kev staggered back and Ollie and I both froze, just for a moment.

"What?" was all our victim could manage.

And as soon as he said that, Ollie pulled a steak knife from his back pocket—one of those small, serrated blades straight from our kitchen's knife block—and lunged at Kev.

Kev jumped back, of course. But I was faster with my wrench than Ollie was with his knife and I did the action hero thing and ran toward him and slid down on my knees in the asphalt (which hurt like fucking Hell), and slammed my weapon into his kneecap.

A sharp yell. "Holy shit! Fuck!" and Kev crumbled. Ollie was already on top of him.

We didn't want to kill him, but we were testing our limits. We were testing Kev's limits.

Ollie jabbed a knife into his arm ("Only the arm, man. I don't want to gut the poor dude. Not that it matters.") while I held him down. I'd never done anything like this before, obviously. Never. Ollie hadn't either. Kev squealed like a pig as Ollie pushed in and pulled out with his knife. And somehow, it was all too easy. Like, who wouldn't do this? Why wouldn't you do this all the time? As Kev squirmed under my weight, the effete little squirmer he was, I felt some great resolve, like the weight of a word, lost on the tip of my tongue, finally materialize. *Yes*, my body screamed.

He tried to get up, he tried to escape. At some point, sawing at Kev's flesh had grown tiresome for Ollie and he threw the knife aside, and seeing a chance at escape, Kev flexed his muscles and jumped up. He was hobbling on one good leg and I was behind him in seconds. I didn't do anything fancy, I just pushed him down.

Kev's arms flailed, comically, as if he were miming a windmill or some shit. And just as I caught up with him, soon Ollie caught up with me. Our victim rolled on his back and looked up at us with horror in his eyes. "*Why are you doing this?*" he cried.

And we looked at each other, me and Ollie, and I don't think we were sure ourselves. Then, one of us kicked him, right in the guts. And then the other did. I'm not sure who went first, but we couldn't help ourselves. There was something so whiny, so pathetic about the mewling creature—Kev of the Quotas— who thrashed back in force and screamed in an empty parking lot. I thought about it for just a moment—why the fuck wasn't anyone coming to help him?—but then my mind drifted to better things. Like the dull, wet impact my shoes made on his stomach. Or the way Ollie's sweat dripped from his forehead onto Kev's white shirt. And then I started to savor our Lordship over our Lord. The disgusting child below us, the wounded animal, the omnipresent, ever-looming, proverbial Enthusiastic Participant.

I didn't know who started delivering the kicks, I really didn't. It was like a dream. Somehow, our actions meshed together as one. We did things without understanding them fully. One kicked and it could have been either of us. But I did know it was I who put my foot on his head.

It was I who looked up at Ollie and gave him that shit-eating, *let's end this fucker* grin.

It was I who pressed down on Kev's head, grinding his ear and cheek into the pavement as his screams got louder and harsher.

Ollie took a step back, and I didn't know if he was smiling or opening his mouth, shocked and appalled.

I used Kev's head as leverage, like a stair step, propelling myself into the air, where for a moment I was weightless. In flight, I leveled my feet out, bringing my knees to my chest. And then, in one harsh movement, I slammed both feet down.

Below me, his skull cracked.

It took us a second to realize what had happened. A long second. And me and Ollie, we both kind of just looked at each other, vaguely aware of some great emotion climbing up through us that we couldn't name.

Finally, he said, "We should go."

I nodded, eyes downcast, avoiding Kev's involuntary twitching with all my might.

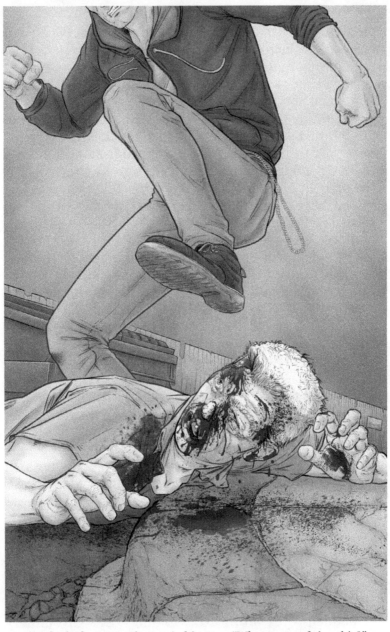

Kev looked up at us, horror in his eyes. *"Why are you doing this?"*

I don't think Ollie and I were sure ourselves.

12

BACK HOME, we didn't talk to each other much. Ollie told me to write everything down, he was going to do the same. As the adrenaline wore off, I felt absolutely sick to my stomach. I felt disgusted with myself. I would've cried if the feelings themselves weren't so large, so difficult to process.

Worst of all, though, I knew that Ollie was upset with me. And that bothered me more than Kev dying did.

I knew he was upset because he pretended he wasn't. "No, it's fine, dude. Shit happens." His voice sounded choked, quiet. "I'm just tired, need some sleep, you know?" He chuckled a little, like a half-hearted sort of cough, and disappeared into his room.

At home, I was reliving the murder. Writing it down, I felt like I was there again, feeling Kev's head break like a cantaloupe. I kept wondering what he felt, what he was thinking as the two losers in his office fucking killed him.

Nausea had overcome me and I threw up several times. I kept listening for police sirens. I figured I made a big mistake, the biggest mistake ever and soon I would be in a cell, because surely, surely—you could not do something like this and have it be okay. That just wasn't possible. Kev was dead and I killed him.

The sun was barely down when I finally got into bed. I couldn't hear Ollie on the other side of the door. I didn't know what he was doing. It worried me that I didn't know what he was doing. I imagined him deciding that his friendship with me had run its course, that I'd taken things too far and he needed an out. He would go live alone and I would be stuck in this stupid two bedroom luxury apartment that I couldn't afford, and somewhere, far away from each other, we'd be counting the seconds on the same clock.

Eventually, I went to sleep, but I wasn't sure when. I tossed and turned for hours until at some point, my eyes closed and they stayed like that, for at least an hour or two. I was asleep, technically, but still so wired that the slightest sound would've sent me leaping from my bed.

In the morning, I was tired, but eager.

Ollie would be the same, I knew. And more than ever, I hoped that he was right. That everything would be reset and Kev would be alright and our memories of the whole thing would be this fleeting thought, a half-remembered melody, a memory sapped of all form and substance. I was up first. I wasn't sure what was supposed to happen. I tried to sort my feelings on the couch, before Ollie woke up.

If I was being honest, I still felt pretty torn up. But the more I thought about it, the more I came to understand my feelings. I wasn't thinking about Kev anymore or what I did to him. That part of it was foggier, or more distant, or both. Me stomping down on Kev's head was like something that happened in a movie, played by actors—irreconcilably distant. I couldn't quite conjure the emotions attached to it, just like you wouldn't be able to feel the emotions of an action hero gunning down dozens of faceless bad guys—it felt more like cinema than experience. I did feel bad, though. I was worried what Ollie would say, how he would feel, just as I was last night, but now those feelings were distinct, separate, no longer intertwined with yesterday's violence.

When Ollie woke up, stumbling out of his room like every other day, he looked at me, nodded, and said, "You're still here. That's good."

"Still here," I said, trying to keep myself together, to be nonchalant.

Ollie brushed the hair out of his face. "How do you feel?"

I shrugged. "I don't know yet. A little weird, I guess."

"Sure, sure."

"You okay?"

"Yeah," he said. "I think things just progressed a little far for me last night. Further than I was ready for at the time. No cops came, right?"

I was confused. "No, no one's been by yet. They'd have been here by now, right? If things hadn't reset?"

"Most definitely. You're safe, don't worry about that."

I breathed in. "We should go to work, check in on...make sure things are alright."

"Yeah, agreed."

We both waited for a moment. I decided to start, to be the straight shooter, lest it loom over us for the rest of the day. "About last night, dude—I don't know what happened."

Ollie put a hand up. "You don't have to explain."

"No—no—I just wanted to say—like, it was all a blur. I didn't know what I was doing. Except, I did sorta. I don't know. I just took things too—"

Ollie shook his head, he cut me off. "No, I should've explained earlier," he said. "I knew what was going to happen, before we did anything. It was my fault." He stopped, taking a breath, rubbing his brow. "You know how I said that the unreal days make it easier to . . . do things differently, I guess? Easier to break routine, skip the decaf, live life on the edge? Well, what I should've said is that they allow less impulse control. When the Tide is high, it's easier to do the things you don't wanna do. Whether that's shitting in the coffee pot or, well, you know."

"Jesus," I said, shamefully alleviated of at least a little guilt. *It wasn't my fault.*

"Yeah."

"But he's okay, right?"

"He's gotta be. Might have a little bit of a bad feeling—like he did something wrong yesterday. You ever get like that? Some days you just wake up and feel off, like you're guilty for something and you don't know why? I sometimes wonder if someone killed me the day before, and it just washed away like a dream."

"I can't believe I did it though."

"When the Tide is high, you're liable to do anything. I'd try not to dwell on it. I was there too. I wasn't much kinder."

"I just feel like shit."

"I bet we'll get used to it."

I laughed. Ollie had that boyish look on his face. He looked mischievous.

"And besides," he added, with a touch of sorrow. "The next Tide doesn't roll in for another month. We're gonna be in a desert. I think we'll have other problems."

My heart dropped. "A month? How do you know?"

He tapped the side of his head. "It happens every so often, you know? The cycle repeats. I've been keeping track of this for like almost a year, and it seems like every seventy-nine days, it starts over. It's like a pattern. Maybe we'll get lucky and I'll be full of shit though. Fingers crossed, right?"

I couldn't stand the thought of what I did to Kev—but now that I had a taste of freedom, I couldn't stand to go back either. "A whole month," I said.

"Yep, thirty-one days from now."

"Jesus Christ," I said.

He sighed, I sighed. We looked at the clock, hoping to catch another second. "Alright," he said. "Let's go to work.

***

We expected Kev to be fine, of course. I mean, there was always that little voice in the back of my head that screamed: *this is all bullshit, what the fuck are you doing*—but having gone in twice now, having seen the blasé reports of the Tidal Reality from Ollie, who didn't seem crazy, but knowledgeable, I had accepted the Tide as part of our lives. A crazy bit of magic that had blessed me thus far, that had made life worth living again. So, I expected to see Kev, because I knew somehow that if he were still dead, I'd already be in jail.

Still, even if I expected it, I felt relief blossoming within me when I saw him. He turned to us, brushed his stupid, generic, white-guy middle-manager haircut to the side and said, "Morning, fellas," as if we hadn't jumped him the night before. "Best get straight to work," he said. "Corporate is beyond stoked at our jump in productivity. They think we can beat our record. You ready for that? You bros up to the challenge?" He had the light and enthusiastic voice of a motivational speaker. It made me grind my teeth.

Kev moved from desk to desk, explaining the new quotas, relishing the word and its thudding musicality each time he said it. Ollie and I sat down and I think we both gulped at the same time. Like a fucking cartoon. We would've laughed about it too, had Kev not been hovering in the middle of the office like some jungle idol.

"He fucking loves this," I said. "He really fucking loves this."

"You should've cut his fucking head off," said Ollie.

"I could've put it on a spike like Vlad the Impaler. We could've paraded it around to ward off the Turks."

"Quotas," came a voice and I turned to see Kev behind me already. "So," he started again, as if tediousness was the remedy to our slacking. "Corporate has been really excited by the progress at this branch—"

"We know."

"God, Kev, we heard you the first time."

"You need to get back to work," he said simply. "That's what we pay you to do."

"Alright, alright."

"Fine, fine."

And then, when he left, we mouthed to each other, "Fuck off."

But, even being the more cavalier of the office, we still

were afraid of losing our jobs. It took me six months to find this shit job. Ollie said he didn't care, but I could tell he did, at least a little. He was the one who suggested the apartment, after all. So, we shut up and we worked and we tried our best to make our jabs when Kev was out of earshot.

By the time five o' clock rolled around, I felt like my eyes had liquefied. The spreadsheet's grid had started to bend and curve. All of the lines were wobbly and the numbers looked to be from a numerical alphabet I could no longer recognize. I rubbed my eyes. I felt like a leaden blanket had fallen over me. In just one full shift, I was lobotomized. Ollie and I went home, tired and depressed, to our "luxury two-bedroom," where we drank and made attempts at small talk.

The next day we woke up and I think we both were thinking the same way—*a new day, new me* sort of thing. We were going to try to be good and do the job we were paid to do, because we thought there was no reason why two reasonably smart people shouldn't be able to do it. Everyone else in the office could do it. They managed to get up every day and do the same thing, every day, and not feel like their head was going to explode. Or rather, that it would be worth it if it did.

We took our deep breaths. We talked about it on the way there. We practiced mindfulness, plugging in our earbuds in unison and listening to YouTube videos that told us to breathe into our toes. We couldn't help but break out into the giggles when we tried it, but we kept doing it anyway, eyes closed, anxiously waiting for our bodies to answer the woman's voice in our ear.

"It might've done something," I said.

"I definitely feel looser," said Ollie.

And we went with that, a sort of bored recognition that maybe it worked, that maybe simply closing our eyes and controlling our breathing would somehow make the next day go by without any sort of terrible agony.

It was fucking stupid, but we had to believe in it.

When we got to work though, nothing was the same.

Kev was sweating, smiling his toothy grin. I thought with some satisfaction that some of those teeth had cracked against the pavement. "Morning, fellas," he said. The same insipid greeting every morning. I wanted to bash his head in. "As you can see, some things have changed around here."

Ollie and I looked around, taking in the new sights as our stomachs dropped low into our bowels. The whole office had been rearranged. The desks had been further separated, turned to odd angles. They formed concentric circles, like a target, with only one pathway between them all, an empty corridor of carpet that led straight to the bullseye—straight to Kev.

"We're trying something different," he said. "A bit of feng shui to get the juices flowing. Let me tell you where your desk has moved to." He pointed Ollie to the outside rim, and then to me—

My blood boiled. My teeth gnashed.

He pointed me to the innermost circle.

"Right in front of me, fella!" he said joyfully.

My heart was racing, and I think Ollie's was too. We exchanged forlorn looks as we moved apart, severed our ties, and went to separate desks. His desk was behind mine by two rows. He couldn't even see me. If I turned around, I'd be talking to Erik. But Erik was right beside Rich. Rich and Erik were friends. I was putting the pieces together. At my desk I looked at Kev, straight at him. I understood.

This was intentional.

13

THE FIRST WEEK was bad enough. Kev had made sure that Ollie and I were entirely separated, like two children who couldn't be trusted near each other. This was insulting, but it also opened our minds to just how crushing boredom could be. In addition to entering long strings of numbers totally meaningless to us into a huge spreadsheet—also meaningless to us—we now had to read and revise the work of our peers. This was Kev's doing. Something to do with the accuracy of our work.

So, every so often, at Kev's will, we'd share files and stare hopelessly at rows and columns filled with numbers, and somehow, we were supposed to find errors, then correct them.

Oftentimes, I wondered if this was all a big joke. And I thought back fondly to the night I killed Kev, to the feeling of sickness I felt after. Because back then, I had felt something. And now, I only felt a dull humming in my head. How could any day feel unreal when all of them felt unreal? In the back of my head, I wondered if when the day arrived, I'd be able to even trust it, such was my detachment. Would I be able to recognize those stupid quirks that somehow made a day not real? Or would they pass over me like everything else? Maybe that was why they passed most people by unnoticed.

Each day I tried to escape further into my own head. And each time, Kev's timer beeped and forced us into a new task, one that required as much attention and immediacy as it required tedium.

Ollie felt about the same as I did.

At night, we'd talk.

"I don't know if I can make it another three weeks."

"If you call out, I'll call out."

"No, I can't call out. Not now."

"Why is that?"

"Just stuff. Reasons. Need the money. Who the fuck cares?"

Ollie had been getting touchier lately. I assumed for the same reasons I had. I changed gears, cracked a beverage. "Now that the office is all fucked up," I began, "how would you do it?"

Ollie raised an eyebrow. "How would I do it? Shit, dude."

"Think about it."

"Okay," he said, and I knew he was brightening up now. "Alright, so I think I'd start by showing up early. That's when Kev shows up, right?"

"I hear he shows up an hour before the drones. Probably to jack off to the melange of despair."

"And of course, who wouldn't?"

"Kev probably makes a whopping forty-eight-k a year. He's essentially made it." Things felt easier now. Better.

"Alright, so I think I'd want to start with Kev, before anyone else gets there. And this time, I'd do it quick. I'd have my gun and I'd just be waiting at his desk. Blow the fucker's brains out. Or better yet, no—neck shot. Have that fucker just gushing blood down the front of his painfully white shirt."

"Neck shots are underrated," I said sagely. "Do you think, with a high enough caliber, or a shotgun or something, you could decapitate someone with a well-aimed neck shot?"

"I'd like to think so," said Ollie, obviously considering the possibility.

"And so what next? Kev's dead, it's an hour before anyone gets there. What do you do?"

"Hide the body."

"There's blood everywhere."

"Well, yeah. But I don't think anyone's going to notice it. I'll wipe up the obvious stuff, I guess. I want everyone to come and just filter into their seats. Like usual. But they'll notice Kev is gone and it'll be sort of like a normal day, I guess. Except, I'll have gone behind them and locked the doors, blocked the fire exits."

"And then what? You gonna jump out of a desk and be like, 'surprise, motherfucker!'?"

He shook his head. "No, I'm just going to put my back into the corner, where no one can get behind me. And then I'm just going to start shooting, until they're all dead."

I nodded, impressed. "Brilliant. I like it. Simple."

"And I'm going to blow apart those ancient-ass computers too."

"Please, every single one of them."

We continued like that for a while. Everything was okay.

"And what about you?" he asked.

"Me? Jeez, does it matter?"

"You asked me and I answered, of course it matters."

"No, I mean—does it matter if I'm the victim or the perpetrator? You know, if you were coming in with a gun, and I died—a glorious death, I might add—what does it matter whether I get to die or get to kill?"

"Oh, so you mean . . . "

I realized Ollie was still trapped in hypotheticals. It was as if he already forgot.

"Well, I mean. It's just a possibility," I said, walking it back. "I'm just saying, if you come in with guns blazing, kill me at the beginning of the day so I don't have to wait for the clock to strike five."

He laughed at this, and he might have been thinking about it, the logistics of making it happen. I was too, of course. I wanted us to be on the same page. My mind was numb, braindead from the shit creek that was my life. I looked at him, a jocular smile on my lips and I felt like I was Dr. Frankenstein, goading my creature to walk. *Yes! Yes! Yes!* "We *could* do it."

"I've always wanted to die in a mass shooting," I said casually. "It's really the closest you can get to dying a Saint."

I'd always been like this, I decided. When I got tired, bored, I always started pushing buttons. At the end of the night, when I was ready for people to leave, was when things always start to get bleak. Red eyes with leaden lids—and a mouth obsessed with incest, murder, and suicide. *You ever hear that brat screaming and just want to push a pillow over its stupid little mouth.* I'd mimic the pillow, the soft struggle of the infant unable to fight me off. My arms would shake slightly, I'd hold my breath as if I were exerting myself in deep focus. And then, inevitably, the new father or new mother would leave. They'd call their cabs or negotiate who would drive and say, "Alright, fine, it's been great. Bye." Leaving me to the couch, self-impressed at my appetite.

I looked to Ollie and I wondered if he understood what any of this meant. He discovered it, after all.

It was his fault, really.

***

Ollie came around to it quickly, but we both had to pretend to not want to do it for a while. That was the sort of dance one had to do with these things. As Kev continued to put our work lives in a vice, it became easier and easier to imagine ourselves going through with it.

"But what about last time?" Ollie said one night, on the way home.

"What about it?"

"It's just . . . with Kev . . . afterward."

"Yeah?"

"You seemed kind of torn up."

"I can barely remember it now," I lied. "I don't think it was as big of a deal as you're making it out to be."

"I've never killed anyone."

"Technically, I haven't either."

He thought about this for a minute. "That's true, I guess. Kev's still walking."

"Unfortunately."

"So, we'd need guns, right?"

"Yes," I said. "That'd be helpful."

"What kind?"

"Whatever we can afford."

"Wait—I have an idea. There's a waiting period, right?"

"I think so."

"What if we put in the application now, and picked them up when the Tide was high. So that the next day, we wouldn't have them anymore and would still have all of our money?"

"Jesus," I said. "That's genius."

Ollie had a knack for what I called Tidal Thinking. He would often come up with clever *what ifs* to leverage the rules of the Tidal Reality. I think now that this is really what he got out of it—what he wanted most to do. Ollie liked to solve problems. For me, our mental gymnastics were pure catharsis—I relished the content of them, the transgression. I reveled in saying the Very Bad Thing. And Ollie might have enjoyed it too, honestly. I think that was the hard part about everything, people were seldom one thing. We compared ourselves to others and said *I'm this* and *you're that* as a way to categorize and contain, but also to explain ourselves. Because the most important part of it wasn't *you're that,* it was *I'm this*. Keeping that in mind—the way I saw it was that while I lived for the catharsis, Ollie lived for the logistics. He loved how's and why's. He was the sort of guy who liked to come up with plans. He was a tactician.

"But seriously, does it matter the type of guns?"

"Just get whatever feels right, I guess? It's your big day, isn't it?"

A dark pall fell over us then and I think the idea of killing people had really gotten into Ollie's head.

"It's alright, dude!" I said, my voice light and airy. I was trying to be fun and enthusiastic. "They're gonna be alright! You said so yourself."

"Yeah, no, I know."

"I bet Kev is gonna give you lots of motivation in the next couple weeks anyways, right?"

He cracked a smile. "Yeah, probably."

I jostled him lightly. I laughed. I wanted to see him do it. I wanted to die in a rain of hot lead—and then, afterward, I wanted my turn. "See? It's not gonna be anything big. Just another experiment. Probably won't even remember it after it happens."

Kev's head cracked under my weight. It slipped as my weight shifted, shearing off the skin of his forehead on the black asphalt.

I swallowed. "And I'll help with anything you need, of course."

"Of course," he said.

***

Throughout the next week, things at work became worse. I tried staring at my screen as a means of escape. I stared holes into the monitor only because Kev kept staring holes into me. Or maybe he wasn't. I didn't know. But it didn't matter if he was, not really. Because I kept *feeling* like he was anyway. Every second of the day, I felt as if I were being watched. Kev would walk the office like a jailer, and I'd try to crane my neck to see Ollie, to share some sarcastic telepathy for just a moment, but there were too many people, too many desks in the way for us to see each other. Isolation took hold of me during work hours and my depression became a sharpened stake upon which I'd fling myself at the beginning of every day, sinking down its shaft for the next eight hours. And then, the next day, I'd do it again.

My only reprieve was at the end of the day when Ollie and I'd go home and drink our beers, order our pizza, and make the same jokes about death and the same plans about killing. This was how we always bonded, and I needed it more than ever now.

On the day before the Tide, I woke up to find Ollie gone, and I had a small bout of panic. My heart thumped in my ears, adrenaline shot through my veins. I was wired, scared, fighting and flighting. *Where was he? What about tomorrow?* I thought. I'd been looking forward to my catharsis, the only thing for which I lived now. It was the only thing that kept my mind working through my endless, pointless labor. I called to him. "Ollie! Ollie?" But the apartment was empty.

When I checked my phone, I felt like crying in relief.

Called out, doctor's appointment. See ya tonight, dude. Tomorrow's the big day.

And that day at work was not good, but it was better.

14

IT WAS AGREED beforehand that Ollie would leave before me. He'd get there first and I was just going to have a front row seat to the whole big thing. I was half excited to see it go down and half excited to get my brains dusted early enough in the day to not have to work through the rest of it. When I pulled up, Ollie's car was already in the parking lot.

I'd done the wrong thing, of course. I came earlier than I said I would. But, I really wanted to sit outside and enjoy my coffee and listen for a gunshot.

The air was strange, the clocks were off, and Jeffrey Masha, somewhere, had woken up and decided to go mad on the air.

There was no sound though, and when the clock struck nine, I wondered if perhaps Ollie had disposed of Kev much earlier. Or if he chose to use a garrote. I'd heard him mention it, at least once. *Hey wouldn't it be crazy if I went up behind and used one of those wires—you know, like in the fucking* Godfather? I had to tell him what it was called. I got out of the car, which felt empty without Ollie. Usually we'd be spending our time in there bullshitting before work, reliving the agony of yesterday while conjuring the agony of the future. We'd wander in at 9:01, on the dot, as a way to wrestle back just a little time for ourselves.

Today though, my legs were jittery. I was excited. I got out of the car and started walking very quickly. I said hi to the people I would say hi to, which was funny—because normally, I never said hi to anyone. I just walked in with Ollie and started bullshitting anew.

But of course, today wasn't like any other day. Today wasn't real. It'd be forgotten, retconned out of existence. So, just as it was easier for me to murder Kev, it was easier for me to greet, easier to come in early, easier to start working.

My hands were shaking on the keyboard. I peered over my monitor, a smile suppressed on my lips.

Kev was gone.

I almost laughed, cheered. *The maniac had done it.*

I spun in my chair, another superfluous action made easier by the Tide—everyone else was here alright. Everyone but Ollie and Kev.

Oh, where could he be hiding?

The whole office sat in their stupid concentric seats and waited for their quotas to be delivered. They chatted idly, drank their coffee, and talked about what they did last night or what football team won or who got laid or who's kid has been acting like a bitch since they turned thirteen. I didn't talk much though, although I loved to talk. I was waiting for the door to open, for us all to dive down, for Ollie to arrive as the triumphant assassin, walking each circle of desks with his pistol or shotgun—I made him not tell me, I wanted it to be a surprise—blowing each of us apart as we cried into the carpet.

The thought exhilarated me. I couldn't talk. I was waiting for my head to be split open. I felt like a defiant sacrifice, being led up the stairs of the pyramid step by step, grinning ear to ear. My dying felt like the greatest bout of rebellion I could imagine. And in some ways, in a world that demanded your time, voluntary slaughter was the only escape.

When the door opened, I nearly leapt.

My heart raced. I kept my eyes straight ahead.

Then, a voice.

"Sorry, the coffee line ran late."

I swiveled in my chair.

Kev.

Alive.

He hadn't done it yet. "Can't believe how many people were out this morning, jeez Louise," he said. He sat down at his desk, right in front of me. "Morning," he said, his eyes burrowing into me. A hint of suspicion, of distrust, of *hate*. I could fucking see it, the smug bastard. Today, he let his mask down, because today was not real. *The bastard hated me.*

And for a second, I wondered if he remembered.

Suddenly, my giddiness subsided and I realized that Ollie had chickened out. I was going to cry. A lump formed in my throat. I felt like I was going to throw up. It was all the pain of having *something* and then having *nothing*. I wanted to die more than ever right then, and I realized how easy it was to cry, how easy it was to lose hope. Because, really, whatever you did, the Tide just pushed you further along in that direction. I felt betrayed, destroyed, utterly hopeless and as soon as I felt like that, it started to happen.

A new door swung open, and I almost didn't turn my head at all. I only looked because Kev looked and every move he made was tied to my own. Kev stood—I looked up. Kev walked the desks—I followed him with my gaze. So, when the bathroom door flung open, and Kev looked, I was probably the second person to notice Ollie with a shotgun in his hands and a pistol strapped to his side. He wasn't wearing camouflage or a trench coat like we previously discussed. He wore jeans and a T-shirt.

I swallowed.

I opened my mouth.

Pure fucking joy raced through my body.

Ollie stood there, his shotgun's black eye staring us down with cool eternity.

He was shaking like a leaf.

His face was twisted up, in pain, it looked like.

I felt like cheering him on, like *come on, man, you can do it. Let 'er rip. It only takes one trigger pull and the Tide will do the rest.* It was a guide, after all, an accelerant—you just need to provide the catalyst. But Ollie was hesitant, he wasn't built for this, I knew it. I knew somehow he wouldn't be able to deliver and by the time he pulled the trigger, the cops would already be here and they'd take him in cuffs.

I expected everyone to rush him, but no, they just stared at him like dumb cattle. I almost wanted them to rush him. Certainly they would, right? They'd jump up out of their seats and all be a bunch of heroes, right? Fuck no. Everyone just turned, their mouths agape, waiting.

And I almost felt like I was the one who should be standing up, getting ready to take him down. Did the Tides persist after they left us? Was this just another branch of the same reality? Was there another timeline where Ollie and I were in jail for killing Kev? Another timeline where Ollie was dead with a memorial plaque where his desk used to be?

Ollie traced our outlines with the gun barrels. Slowly. He was stalling. I thought about being the hero. I thought about dying first. I thought about ducking down now and playing a game of hide and seek with my best friend. We all thought about this shit, right? How could you not? You were in the workplace and then you saw it on the news and you wondered what would happen if you fought back, or ran, or hid. You imagined the shooter's boots on the ground, walking past your hiding place as you covered your mouth and tried not to breathe so hard.

But, in reality, the whole frozen-with-fear thing happened. They just sat there. They thought it was joke. Ollie, I thought, was realizing this at the same time, because it wasn't easy to kill people who did nothing.

I cleared my throat. I was ready to be what he needed me to be. Fear filled my body, but the Tide kept me moving. My legs flexed. I started to stand.

Then, I heard Kev speak. "Ollie, what are you doing?" he asked.

"He's got a gun," someone else said, as if they were just now realizing it.

"What are you doing?" asked another.

Questions rang up like a chorus and eventually they just repeated his name. "Ollie?" "Ollie?" "What's wrong, Ollie?" "Is this some sort of joke, Ollie?"

Kev was the one to stand up, to walk toward him, his hands up, as if he were meeting a dangerous animal. Part of me hurt, seeing Kev stand up first, taking the role of hero. Kev deserved nothing but a nameless grave. But no, now he'd be talked about in the newspapers and on TV. He'd be the sort of hero the media loves—a tragedy proliferated in social media posts and chain emails.

"You don't want to do this, Ollie," he said. "You don't want to hurt anyone. Maybe we can talk about this. Nothing's so bad, man. We can talk."

I felt sick watching him try to placate him. I looked at Ollie, waited for his eyes to dart to mine. He'd see me. He'd look at me, I knew he would. *Just look at me. Look at me. Look at me, Ollie.*

And then he flicked his eyes toward mine and I could see his watery pupils from across the room. He was so scared. I like to think, as Kev approached him, I gave him strength. I nodded, I smiled, I comforted him. He saw someone he knew and suddenly, when Kev was just an arm's distance from the barrel of his shotgun, he pulled the trigger.

Ollie's arms jerked from the kickback. I wasn't sure if he'd ever shot a gun before. I thought the shotgun was gonna fly out of his hands—it almost did, I could see it slipping out, just barely, from his wet, sweaty fingers. The roar of it was deafening. My ears hurt so bad that I wondered if I'd been shot straight through the head and was dying. *Was this how it felt to die?* We all watched Ollie at first though. The gun's loud blast, it's flash of orange light, its user's contorted expression—we were so focused on Ollie that we barely noticed Kev, his chest cavity open, limp on the floor.

And then, I imagined we all had the same thought. Even I—who knew what was going to happen—who *dreamed* of this finally happening—got lost in the momentum. Suddenly, fight or flight kicked in and everyone in the office was scrambling for an exit. I was with them, I was clawing for a place amongst them. What happened to me? Out of nowhere, I felt the ultimate fear of being a man about to die. I turned my head for a moment and saw Ollie standing by the restrooms with his gun, his brows furrowed and I was really thinking about it in two ways: part of me wanted him to stop, wanted *us*, the good guys, to survive; the other part wanted him to keep shooting, to end every single one of us. But we were moving so fast. There was no way he'd get us.

Then, he fired again.

Beside me, Kayla fell to the floor. That was how it happened, you know? No one got blasted back like in the movies, they just sorta fell. Like, one second they were alive and then the next second they were dead. Point and click—where life once had been, it was no more. Kayla was gone, just like that. Erased from consciousness. Or maybe she wasn't, maybe her spine had just been severed by the buckshot and she was hearing all this, feeling the feet trample on her body as we tried to escape.

"The doors are locked!" someone shouted, frenzied. "The doors are locked!" And just like that we were a school of fish, moving as one as Ollie pumped another round and fired again and again and again. Around me—in front of me, behind me—people fell, eyes rimmed with fear. They marveled and agonized over the blood on their clothes. Sometimes, after they fell, they still moved—quivering, cold, and disquieted till the end.

Once the shooting started, it probably lasted only a minute. One minute between the first shot and Kev dying and then four more. I heard the clack of the shotgun hitting the floor and turned to see Ollie, standing like a statue, reaching for a pistol strapped to his side. His face wasn't twisted anymore. He seemed to have reached some sort of zen-like trance, where violence had become a natural force, a gravitational experience. He flicked the safety and took aim.

Three successive cracks, each duller, less vibrant than the last—each still ringing in my ears. The first sounded like some great seamstress in the sky ripping the threads from reality. Loud, mighty, defining. The sort of sound that changes your life. The second was a roar, a war cry—a *fuck you*. Weak, mealy human catharsis. Vocal cords raising Hell against the void. By the time his finger squeezed the trigger for the third time, it only sounded like a gunshot.

Two more fallen, but not dead. One miss and a shattered window. We all thought the same thing.

Somewhere, distantly, I became aware of police sirens and joy leapt in my heart. We all started to run toward the window, straight out from two stories up; the survivors made their leaps of faith into the bushes. I heard cracks and pops as they hit the ground.

And Ollie, blankly, kept firing. Not fast or slow, but at a steady rate, only breaking to discard an empty clip. I was almost to the door, I was going to be a survivor. I heard my heart in my ears. This whole thing, it was nothing like what I imagined. It was nothing like what I thought it was going to be. I pushed someone out of the way, screams sounded all around me. Someone must have tripped. Someone must have slipped in blood. Someone must have fallen and hugged an old, cold friend.

I felt a hand on my shoulder. Firm, insistent. It turned me around.

Coworkers scattered further, either through the window or below desks. The sirens grew louder. I was looking in Ollie's wet eyes.

He didn't say a word. He just lifted the pistol to my forehead. I forgot to close my eyes. I barely heard the sound.

15

DEATH WAS NOTHING. Death was peace. It was the absence of all. When I woke up, I pitied consciousness. I pitied all of Ollie's victims who would not get to experience the void forever. When I woke up, I missed its absence. And then, soon, the feeling drifted away. Because you couldn't remember death. You just couldn't.

***

Ollie didn't get up, not when I did. I figured I'd let him sleep.

I peered into his room and saw him still in the bed and figured he was worn out—and rightly so. He'd had a big day.

I flexed my fingers, rolled my shoulders. I traced the outline of where there should've been a bullet hole, right in the middle of my forehead. I had to get used to having a body again. It was an interesting sensation. I wondered if Ollie had to do that too, after his suicide.

While my body still felt like a stranger, I began to make breakfast. I was cheerful. I clanked each pan against the burner. I turned on music. I danced! I'd never been a fucking dancer once in my life, and here I was dancing. I felt as if we'd gotten away with something incredible. We were sneaky. We were *villains*. I laughed as I flipped an egg and thought about the laundry list of dead who were reported on the news the night before. Reporters had to stand in front of our office, their faces serious and stressed. Men and women in blankets, the survivors, ushered to ambulances behind them. And then, the next day—all of it was gone.

I had bacon, eggs, and hash browns ready for when Ollie got out of bed. I hadn't even realized he was behind me, yawning and rubbing his bloodshot eyes.

"Hi," he said.

"Morning, sunshine. I made breakfast."

"Thanks," he said.

Everything was already on the plate. I set him up at the bar counter, eager to hang on every word. I wanted to know what happened after he scrambled my brains. I wanted to know what to expect when the Tide came again.

He looked tired, though. Like he hadn't rested at all. He was rubbing his temple. His eyes glinted in the morning sunlight. Weakly, he reached for a piece of bacon.

"So?" I asked.

He shrugged.

I tried again. "How'd it go?"

"Didn't sleep," he said. His syllables were hoarse, strained.

"No?"

He was looking down at his plate then he was looking up at me. It was, as if, overnight, he'd been beaten. Slammed back and forth between forces bigger and heavier and meaner. Physically, he was fine. He was the same Ollie. But, those eyes revealed bruises.

He coughed. He trembled as he took another bite. "You know what happens when you don't sleep? When the Tide pulls out but you're still awake?"

Finally, we were getting to it. "No, what?" I asked, a little too eagerly.

"It feels like you're being wiped. Scrubbed. But only on the outside. I was lying awake, because I couldn't sleep—"

"You didn't kill yourself?"

He shook his head. "No, I surrendered." He said it dreamily, as if he half-remembered it. "I couldn't sleep because they kept me up all night for questioning. I mean, I couldn't have slept anyways though. I just sat there while they screamed at me. They had a television on, I think they wanted me to know what happened, to see what happened. Did you know Erik has kids? I saw them on the news. I—I—"

"They're fine," I said. "Everything reset. Nothing happened, right?"

"Right, I guess." He took a sip of coffee. "Well, I was just frozen. Stuck in interrogation. And I was scared, honestly. I didn't realize how scary it was actually going to be. They named everyone I killed. And I was just sitting there and there was no clock in the room, so I had no idea when it started to happen, but I began to feel tingly, cold. You know that feeling you get when you're trying to fall asleep, but you keep feeling like you're falling and your body just sort of jerks awake, like you're bracing for impact? It was like that. But a very long fall. And I was falling, as I felt this sort of scrubbing, this cleaning, this acid wash. I was in two places at once. I could feel my bed behind me. And in front of me, I could see the detectives. My eyes were pinned open. My heart was slamming, man. And slowly, they just started to fade in front of me. Their voices became all jumbled up, like they were speaking a different language. And it was like I was living a dream, because it was the same sort of thing as when you dream someone is talking to you, but you can't remember what they're saying or what they actually sound like—you just innately have a *sense* of what they're saying. I knew they were telling me I was bad, that I was evil, that I deserved to be buried in a hole for a thousand years. That the families I destroyed would never forgive me. That the specter of my actions would haunt them for the rest of their lives." He took a deep breath, as if he were gasping for air. I wanted to shake him. "When I got back to my room, I couldn't do anything. I just sat there, still."

I didn't know what to say. "But you'll feel better in a day or two, right?"

He shrugged. No answer.

"They're all gonna be fine."

He stopped eating. Leaned on his hand. I was waiting for

him to rebut me, but instead he just waved his hand. "I'm going back to bed," he said. "I didn't get much sleep."

***

We both called out of work, separately. We were both processing what happened, in different ways. That was how I justified it.

But I was confused, because we were miles apart.

Because I didn't feel bad. How could I? No one really got hurt. They'd wake up to live their same shitty lives the next day and the next and the next. And so would I.

I paced around the living room. I wanted so desperately for Ollie to wake up, big smile on his lips and come out and talk to me, to share in the excitement. I was bouncing off the walls. I couldn't help it.

I died.

I experienced death.

How did you come back from that?

I went out for a bit, just to walk, to get some fresh air, to burn some of the nervous energy I'd accumulated. Everywhere I went, I saw people caught like flies on sticky paper. They were buzzing away in their routine, going nowhere fast as they slowly died. They played with their kids, strained smiles on their lips. They checked their mail, eyes glazed over at another day of junk mail. Some of them clocked in at work, subconsciously aware that they were selling time, their most precious commodity. I shook my head. I really hated it. I hated it so much. I hated *me* so much, because I'd been caught in the same cycle.

But Ollie helped me change that.

My mind kept circling around to the same fact: I wished I could be who I was yesterday, forever. A victim of violent crime, a name. A name to mourn. There'd be national conversations about what happened to me. *They were friends, apparently. That's what his coworkers said. They lived together. We may never know what caused the shooter to snap . . .*

But, sure, they'd talk more about Ollie. They wouldn't

want to, of course. They'd keep paying lip service to me and the other corpses. They'd talk about how, just maybe, they shouldn't use the shooter's name in the media. They'd say: "We should be remembering the victims." But that's a laugh, and even walking around the city, watching all the drones fly their set paths, I thought it was funny. It pleased me that somewhere, my dead body was part of some cosmic joke. Because of course we didn'twant to remember the victims.

We didn't give a shit about victims.

Never had, never will.

We cared about the transgressor. The One Who Dared to Go There and Do That. The victims represented a *break* in routine. Dying was but a hiccup in a normal life. Killing was *breaking* the routine—it was bending reality to your own will, making it in your image. We, humans, had a knack for religion, we had a knack for believing in a god. It didn't matter whether it was a God of Love or God of Death—so long as it leveraged absolute control.

So, yeah—I was pleased with having my routine broken. I was happy to be the me who was unceremoniously gunned down. I had all the celebrity of a sacrifice.

But the next step was to be Ollie. The God of Death. The Changer. The Revoker of Lives.

I put my hands in my pockets.

I tried to look calm.

I tried to look like the rest of them—stuck in a diving plane, no escape hatch.

When I went back to the apartment, our *luxury* two-bedroom, I knocked on Ollie's door right away, with every intention to ask him when the next Tide was. All I got was silence.

After a minute, I opened the door and peeked in, slowly, discreetly, as this was a rule between us, that we would not enter each other's rooms without permission.

And then I opened the door wide. "Ollie?" I said to an empty room.

Ollie was gone.

16

LIVING ALONE WAS a funny thing. Because, yeah, I'd done it before. Most of my adult life had been spent living alone. But, it wasn't until my time with Ollie that I felt like a unit. You know, like, as a kid, you weren't just living somewhere, you had a home. You had other people you talked to everyday, who gave a shit about you. Living with Ollie was more like having a family, a brother or a cousin or something, someone you connected to in a way that made any place you settled home. So yeah, I'd been living alone a long time, but after turning the apartment upside down, looking for my friend—no, my family—that was the first time I truly felt alone.

Ollie's room was a mess, but from the glimpses I'd had in the past, that was par for the course. The dude lived in a perpetual state of chaos. He thrived on it. He had oily paper plates on his floor, empty beer and soda cans stacked high next to his computer. Papers and USB cords and everything else tangled together in a nest on the floor. His bed was a mess of twisted covers, the mattress itself sat diagonally on the frame. The sheets were wadded up in a ball on the floor.

Whenever I caught glimpses of Ollie's room, I saw his mind. Or, his *real* mind. Not the one he showed me. The one he showed me was a mirror of my own, and fittingly, the rest of the apartment was clean, normal. Ollie was a chameleon. He'd be able to relate to anyone, empathize effortlessly.

I saw him before with Erik and he just seemed so natural

talking about sports, and I asked him about it later, I thought he was making a joke of it, like he was mocking them. But Ollie looked at me as if I was an alien. "I know about sports," he said with a shrug. "I know about a lot of things."

Standing in his room, I said, "So, this is Ollie," hoping that his name would evoke his presence. But it didn't. The room was empty. No note, no text, no explanation—just gone, as if he never existed.

**

Ollie was just blowing off steam, I decided. He'd be back. He needed to go run off some of that emotion or something. I'd seen Ollie go on jogs before. It could happen.

So, I just did my best to be interesting and comfortable when he came back. I was going to comfort him. I was going to have his back, because we were friends and that was what friends did. I threw on the television and grabbed a six pack of beers, determined to drink them all before he returned. I wondered if he'd find it endearing—me getting drunk all alone while he was out. I figured he'd want to sit down and have some too, and when he'd settled down and the vividness started to dissipate, he'd maybe be back to his old self. He'd want to watch TV with me, he'd want to get drunk too.

Well, I did get drunk. Plenty drunk. It didn't stop at the six pack. I was pouring myself cups of liquor and the whole time I had my eye on the door. I was just waiting, you know? Waiting for Ollie to come back in. I kept listening for his footsteps on the other side of the door. Some shuffling, some nervous breathing, the clang of keys. But nothing. I got drunk and Ollie never showed.

**

It was night when I passed out. I was delirious. A couple times I thought I saw him, but I couldn't move. I might have just been dreaming, or imagining it. I thought I saw him walk in for a minute and walk past me, like a ghost of ritual, going to his room for bed. I blinked and he was gone. But it was then that I got up too, as best as I could, to go to bed myself.

I was so drunk I already felt the beginning of the hangover. Still, I forced my liquid body to peer back into Ollie's room, to make sure he hadn't snuck in.

Nothing, empty.

I slept.

***

In the morning, I considered the very real possibility that Ollie might not come back. I called out of work again and sat at home and tried to decide where he might have gone. Ollie didn't have any family nearby. He might have money and be staying at a hotel, but I didn't know for sure.

I kept putting pen to scratch paper, with the full intention of discovering something about Ollie. Instead, whenever I did, I found myself scratching out numbers.

I was going over my sick days, the totality of my paid time off.

"Really, I could call out for the next week, if I wanted," I said aloud. "Usually, he said they're once a week, or something close to that." I was muttering. "I could call out until the next one. I'll just have to keep my eyes open."

***

A week passed and Ollie never showed. I had his number, yeah. And I called him a lot. I never got an answer. I went to work most days, but each time I did, I was cured of any renewed desire to participate. Kev and the others made jokes about Ollie being gone. Brown bag flu, they said. Like he'd just been partying and feeling ill and that's why he wasn't showing. Kev seemed more annoyed by it than the others. "Well, if he misses much more . . . " he'd say, trailing off. We knew what he meant.

Each day, I counted the seconds on the clock. I watched for Jeffrey Masha on the television, I made snap judgments every day, guessing how long I'd have to wait for the Tide.

I came up with nothing.

Nothing I could be sure of. I lost count too easily. I got distracted by my own shit. I could never remember if the things people did were normal or not. That was Ollie's territory, he was the observer. I wasn't good at that shit.

I was stewing, internally screaming at the boredom of my life.

Every day I was locked into a coma, my body a vegetable, my mind fully alive and rattling its cage.

***

The end of the month came and my sorrow had transformed to hate.

Rent was due, after all.

I lived paycheck to paycheck, just like everyone. My meager savings weren't more than a couple hundred bucks. It took everything I had to plug the hole that Ollie left.

I really started to hate him.

I was out of sick time.

I had to work.

I thought about a new job, something I could love.

But there were always more Kevs. Always more button-ups and bland coworkers—there was an endless amount of everything I hated. And there was no Ollie.

My last beer sloshed into my gullet. It warmed me.

I sighed, sniffed, rubbed something wet from my eye. I had to go to bed. I had work in the morning.

***

Where the fuck was he?

I was staring at a spreadsheet. My brain folded in on itself as I entered digits into squares. Kev stood over me, hmm-ing with approval.

"Killing it, fella," he said.

I couldn't wait to kill him again.

Whenever Kev talked to me, I remembered the time I crushed his skull against the pavement. It was a satisfying memory. When stuck in a concentric circle, there wasn't much else for me. Ollie was gone still, three weeks gone.

But what hurt most was that I knew I'd already missed several Tides. I must've. They were right there, right in front of me, and I had no idea. That was what hurt the most. That I could've escaped, for just a day, but didn't.

***

At lunch, Erik sat beside me. "Sandwich? Nice, cool," he said.

I nodded, pretending not to listen. I didn't usually take my breaks inside, but for some reason, I didn't see a point to leaving anymore. Eating indoors was just another way to accept that this place was my casket.

"So, dude, how you been?"

Erik was older than me, a father, a jocular sports fan with a gray-flecked beard. He had strong arms and a straightforward manner of speaking.

"Okay," I lied, not looking up.

He breathed deep, expanding his barrel chest. "Sure, man, sure." He stretched his arms, cracked his knuckles. "It's just," he started, "me and some of the others have been talking. You seem *not*-okay. A little off. Maybe a little down?"

I looked at him blankly. "What do you mean?"

"Oh, well, you know. Look, man, it's none of my business—but we're worried about you. Like, really worried."

"What have I been doing?"

"You just seem off."

"What does that mean though?"

"It means that you're acting differently."

"You barely knew me in the first place though. This is just how I act, maybe."

He balked. "Oh, c'mon, man. I knew you better than that. I went to your party, didn't I? I used to hang with Ollie every now and then. He'd talk about you. We've talked here and there at work too. Let's not pretend we're strangers, okay?" His voice was soft, personable. I almost caved.

"I'm fine. Really, I am."

"Okay," he said. "Just, if you're not fine, know that people around here are willing to talk, okay?"

"Got it, thanks."

"How's Ollie?"

I shrugged. "Vanished on me. Dude was always sort of a flake."

He nodded slowly. "Got it," he said, as if that explained everything. "Alright, then. Well, if you ever need anything . . . "

"I know where to go."

Another week wasted, another Tide missed, and it seemed like all of them came to talk to me in turn. They each said their piece, as if they were bringing gifts to a God of Death, offers of humility and kindness. "Do you want to go out this weekend, maybe?" "I have some extra food, if you're interested." "Are you going to move?" "If you need any help with it, let me know."

They all said what they needed to say, and I was just so fucking bored of it. Just bored to death.

And it was then that I knew what to do. Alone in the break room, phone in my hand, Ollie's number staring back at me.

Im gonna kill every one of them when the tide comes in tomorrow.

I stared back at my phone.

Then: three dots.

Wait wait wait lets talk.

Okay.

17

I **REALLY JUST** thought I won, right there.

I was sitting outside, wire chair, drinking a coffee. It was midday and I couldn't really tell if everything was right anymore. But it was right enough. I knew I was going to get my friend back.

Sure enough, right on time, he showed up. He suggested a public meeting, I didn't know why. He'd gotten jumpy, I guessed. I stood up when he came toward me. "Ollie," I said. "Long time, no see." He didn't smile when he saw me, just nodded.

"How are you?"

"Good," I said. "Great."

"Sorry, about—you know." He kept looking down at his feet, like he couldn't stand to look at me.

"Are you coming back to the apartment?"

He shook his head fast. "No," he said as he sat down with me.

I swallowed. I felt the knife in my chest, twisting. "Do you want to tell me why?"

And that was when something happened that I just couldn't have expected. Ollie laughed. Loud, mirthless laughter. He was laughing at me. And when he saw my face, his smile faded to a grimace. "Wait," he said. "You really don't know?"

"No. I guess not."

I felt my posture get rigid. My back straightened. I was

puffing out my chest. Blood rushed in my ears. He was trying to make me feel stupid. I'd never felt stupid in front of Ollie before. I didn't like it.

He just shook his head. He sighed. "Do you want to know where I've been the last month?"

"Sure," I said, keeping the syllable tight and ice-cold.

"I checked myself into a place. A—jeez—I don't want to sound melodramatic, but like a mental hospital. For people going through stuff, tragedy, suicidal ideation, et cetera."

"Really now." Despite the coolness of my response, I hadn't expected that. Ollie was always very well put-together. He never let an inkling drip of any mental illness, at least not to me.

"Yeah," he said, gaining momentum. "It was really good. Really set me on the right track. It made me realize a lot of things, a lot of things about how I've lived my life. Or, rather, how my situation and biology have forced me to live my life." He paused for a moment. "Maybe," his voice was like a whisper, a choke, "you should consider going too."

It was my turn to laugh. "Why the fuck would I do that?"

"Because you need it. It'll help."

"Is this about what happened at work? The last Tide?"

"Of course it is!" he yelled. Ollie had his hands up, he was ready to grab me by the collar. He looked around, self-conscious. He put his hands back to his side. Then, half to himself, "How could it be about anything else?"

"None of it was real though. None of it mattered, right?" I was getting tired of this already. I didn't understand why he was being like this.

"It was real for me."

"Yes, and then everything resets and it's fine."

"I *killed* people, dude. I hurt them. I'm a murderer."

"But—"

He cut me off. "But nothing. That shit doesn't wash away. It stains you. I can't sleep at night, man. I keep thinking about—about—about what happened. What I did. I keep seeing their bodies, falling. Just falling flat, like something inside of them got extinguished. Whatever fire that makes people alive, snuffed in an instant. I did that."

"You did," I said. "And I want to do that too. I never got my turn."

"You got Kev," he said. "That's enough."

"Kev didn't count."

"Weren't you beat up after you did it?"

I shrugged. "Maybe a little. But it passes. Just like it'll pass for you. You need to come back to the apartment."

"No," he said, "stop." He had his hands up again, warning me. "It's not a safe place for me, right now. I hate to do this to you, but I'm not coming back. I know it's a lot, but I spent all my money on the hospital. It's gone. But I'll be happy to send you a portion of my rent or whatever when I get a new job."

I shook my head. I leaned back. I tried to swallow my rage. "You really fucked me over."

"I know, I'm sorry."

"Are you?"

"Look, dude," he said, starting slowly. I was getting angrier, because he kept talking to me like I was some sort of a child. Like I was stupid. He started every sentence as if I *just wasn't getting it.* "I needed to do this for myself. To be right again. I've always had problems, you know? Not big problems, but just enough small problems that shit was hard. Everything we've done with the Tide . . . it just made shit worse for me. I can't be that person anymore. I want to forget it exists."

"What?"

"As far as I'm concerned, The Tide doesn't exist. It can't exist, for my own health and safety."

"But you were there." I was speaking too fast, I was too excited. "I remember. You had the shotgun, and you were just tearing through everyone. Kev too, especially Kev. You fucking floored him, man. You ended that motherfucker. It was the greatest thing I'd ever seen."

He sighed. "If that's true, that's really fucking sad, man."

"I wanna have a turn."

More sighs, more consternation, more of Ollie blue-balling me out of some newfound "inner peace."

"C'mon, it's only fair. I wanna do it."

He looked past me, like he was staring off forever. I waited, while his eyes went glossy and his mouth went slack. Finally, he said, in that same irritatingly slow voice, "I had a feeling you'd want to. That it'd come to this."

Finally, we were getting somewhere. "Well, no shit. We've talked about it for, like, ever."

Ollie: still staring into space. "What if I refused? What are you going to do then?"

This is where I knew I had him. Ollie was smart, but he wasn't that smart. He stepped right into my trap. I smiled. "I'll just guess," I said.

This snapped him out of it. "Guess?"

"Yep, guess. Is it tomorrow? Does it matter? I can get a gun by tomorrow. I can steal one the morning of, I don't care."

"But you don't know if it's tomorrow."

"Nope," I said. And I think he was finally seeing my point. "I don't care. It's my turn. You can either help me kill a lot of people when there's no consequences or you can let me spin the ol' roulette wheel and take a chance. Either way, it's going to happen. It has to happen at this point. I need this, man."

I sounded desperate, but it worked.

"Fuck," he said, tears rimming his eyes again. "Fuck. Fuck."

"When's the next Tide, Ollie?"

He looked scared, trapped. He was thinking. He shook his head back and forth, as if he were trying to shake away an awful idea. I didn't know why I liked him so much right then, he was so pathetic.

"You're just never gonna want to stop, huh?" he asked, finally.

"Not as long as I live in this world," I said.

"Okay," he said, finally. His voice quivered. "The day after tomorrow."

I nodded, I breathed out. Relief flooded me. "Okay."

18

OLLIE DIDN'T TEXT me the next day, but I didn't care
about that. Because really, I meant what I said. I was
excited about something and I wasn't going to let
anything get in the way. I felt like I had given myself
permission, finally, to act. And really, nothing else mattered.
The Tide didn't matter, not really. The Tide would only allow
me to act more than once. But you know what they said: live
every day like it's your last. So, that was what I did.

It wasn't hard for me to find weapons. My father was a
hunter, after all. I hadn't been home for over a year and all I
had to do was stop by unannounced and get to chatting.

I never felt at home with my family, but still, I walked up
and knocked.

My Mom opened the door. She'd gotten older since I'd
last seen her. My father stood behind her, a couple feet back.
We left on ill terms last time, but it was alright. I could play
along.

"Mom," I said, embracing her. "Dad," I said.

He threw my handshake away and it was as easy as that.
He pulled me in. "Son," he said. "It's been too long."

"Too long," I confirmed.

They led me into the house, pictures surrounding me like
mirrors out of time. There I was as a child, there I was as a
teenager, oh look—there I was as a graduate.

"You want some coffee?"

"Yes, love some."

"Cream, sugar?"

"Black is fine."

"Alright, hon. Give me a second."

Me and my father were left alone and he was staring at me intently, studying me. Finally, with a sigh, he said, "Jesus. I'm so old."

"Ah, don't say that."

He gestured to me. "You're a young man now." He shook his head. "It's just crazy to see."

"People grow up."

"That they do."

We sat there for a moment, just thinking about that, I guess. The inevitability of it all, of everything. The fucking, living, and dying that make up the circle of life. And me, the Great Disruptor of the Circle.

Mom came back in with coffee and we all sipped and discussed trivialities.

"How's work?" she asked.

I felt like a machine—for each input, I had an output. "Great," I said, because you always had to respond in the affirmative. You always had to shield people from your own discontent. Depression became "tired," work became "great." It was just how it went.

"Still digging it, huh?" said Dad, musing to himself. "You always were a wiz with computers."

"You were," said Mom nodding. "You were always doing something on one of those things. I never could understand it, not at all."

"Same, that just passed us by, I guess. But you work with computers now, you went to school for it and everything."

"Well, yeah," I said. "I mean, it's not the same sort of stuff I went to school for."

Dad waved a hand. "At least you have a job. Not everyone does."

"Right," I said, my teeth grinding. "You're right."

"My friend Amy, remember Amy, right? Well, Amy's son

is still looking for a job. He's had to work at a grocery store. It's been over a year too, poor guy. He's still looking though. You just can't ever give up," said Mom.

"Right," I said.

A long pause, a round of coffee sips. "So, what are you doing today? What brings you by?" said Dad.

He was looking old, just like he said. His beard was gray and scruffy, his eyes were tired—but not depressed tired—just old tired. Like, he'd been alive too long.

I said, "Well, I have some buddies, a couple buddies from work—and we were thinking of going shooting."

"Shooting? Like target shooting?"

"That's right."

"Where at?"

"One of the guys has an old farm, out in the country. No one around for miles."

"Out North?"

"Northwest."

"Ah," he said. "Must be beautiful."

The lies came out of nowhere. "It is," I said. "At least I've heard."

I didn't even have to ask.

"Well, jeez, you wanna bring the Winchester? Or maybe one of the handguns? Haven't used either in forever, they probably need to be fired every so often."

"Oh man, I haven't seen those in years," I said, appealing to his nostalgia. "I remember those from when I was a kid, back when you used to take me hunting."

"Ha," he coughed. "I always thought you hated those trips."

"You hate everything when you're a teenager."

He nodded, as if he knew this was true. "I suppose."

"Distance makes the heart grow fonder, I guess."

And he bought into it right away. "You're absolutely right about that one. My Dad used to take me out to the Indian casinos, all the time. He thought I liked to watch him play cards with his buddies. Hated it. But now—now that he's gone, anyways—wouldn't trade those times for the world."

"Just be careful now," said Mom, chiming in. "Don't be drinking. It's not safe to be drinking with guns around."

"They're all well-acquainted with the rules," I said. "We'll be really safe."

This seemed to placate both of them.

For the next hour, I spent my time trading memories. I assisted them in coloring my youth as normal and happy. I grabbed a paint brush and went to work, they just told me what to paint. Dad was no longer abusive, he was just a bit of a hard-ass, we laughed about that. The time he beat me, out of some irrational hatred of seeing me on the computer, became a joke. A nice *remember when?*—a reminder of purer, simpler times. Eventually, I told them what they wanted to hear—that I loved them and they were perfect.

And as I got up, my Dad played his part perfectly. "Wait now, let's not forget those guns."

"Oh yeah, of course," I said. "I almost forgot."

"Do you need ammo?"

"If you have it."

"Oh yeah, I can load you right up. Your buddies are going to get a kick out of these. They might think they're relics, but jeez, if they don't hold up. Beautiful machines."

"I'm sure they'll love them," I said. "They're big gun nuts."

He walked away and my mother asked, when he was out of earshot. "Are you really okay?"

I swallowed. Nodded. "Yep," I said. "Great. Just tired."

***

That night, I dreamed, I was sure. For the little sleep I got, I was sure I dreamed.

19

I WOKE UP EARLY, but Ollie had gotten up earlier. I twisted out of bed and looked at my phone, and to my delight, his name was already on the front of it.

I'll be over soon.

The message was sent just ten minutes before, which excited me. Because I was going to see my friend. Seeing Ollie in the luxury two-bedroom apartment that he decided we needed, was bringing with it waves of nostalgia. Those were the best days of my life, I realized. Me and Ollie, drinking, talking shit, watching movies—escaping together.

I was already dressed when the doorbell rang. I composed myself. I closed my eyes, breathed, tried to stall my jackhammering heart. "Alright," I said. "This is it. This is the big day."

I opened the door. "Ollie, good morning."

"Good morning."

He was dressed casually. In the same clothes he always wore, just a T-shirt and jeans. He looked tired, just like me. He stood stiffly in my doorway.

"Come on in," I said. "Please, come on in."

Ollie surveyed the place silently.

"I've got coffee brewing," I said. "If you want some."

A pause. A breath. "Sure." Defeated.

I got him a cup, and myself one too. "Sit," I said. "Sit. We've got plenty of time."

He sat on the couch and sipped his coffee. He stared at

me blankly. "I came here one last time, because I want you to reconsider."

My teeth ground. I could almost feel the enamel turn to dust, then mud in my mouth. "Why?" I said.

"Because—because it's not right. I feel stupid saying it, but it's just not right."

"No one's going to die though, right?"

"I mean, we don't know that. We don't know how the Tide works."

"So what? Some dude I've never met dies in a branching reality and I'm supposed to give a shit?"

"Yes, that's what I'm telling you. You're supposed to give a shit."

I shrugged, frustrated. "Well, I don't."

"I know, that's the problem." He stopped, caught his breath, tried again. "I know why you want to do this. Because it's the same reason I went and did it. I'm not trying to moralize you, okay? I'm not like some moral paragon or anything. I did bad things too. I egged you on when I shouldn't have. After Kev died, the first time, I should have ended everything. But I didn't, and I guess that's why we're here now. I'm just telling you, man, what you're doing . . . it's not real—"

"I know it's not real."

'No, fuck you, man—it's not that. It's not real catharsis. It's more escapism, dude. That's all we ever did, every second of the day, was try to escape."

"No shit."

He sighed. "Do you wanna hear what I have to say or not? Because I want to get it out, before I help you, because maybe it'll change your mind."

I drank. "Okay, sure, say your piece." I was already imagining the cold metal in my hands, the blood spurting from open wounds.

"Look man, have you ever read *Candide*? By Voltaire?"

"No."

"Right, well, you weren't an English major, I guess, huh? Well, it's a pretty short book, maybe you'd like it. It's basically this sorta, I don't know, satirical adventure story. Picaresque, is what we called it."

"What does that mean?"

"It means, like, one thing just happens after the other. Like: this happened, and then this happened, and then this happened."

"Sounds like life," I said.

"Well, maybe. I don't know about that. But at the end of the book the sort of famous scene is, after all of these adventures that sort of make fun of intellectuals, people in power, and whatever, someone basically asks him, what do we do now and the main dude says: 'we must cultivate our garden.'"

I didn't understand what he was trying to say. "And?"

"It means we got to focus on the shit close to us. To make a better life. I was thinking about that a lot, you know? That's why I had to leave."

I felt my grip on the coffee mug tighten. "You're saying I wasn't a part of your better life?"

"No," he said. "You were actively making my life worse."

We stared at each other for a while after that. Mine heated, his blank.

"It was just something to think about, you know," he said. "Before this goes where it'll eventually go."

I couldn't hold it in anymore. "Fuck you, dude! You started this! You were the same as me! Don't try and turn this into—into—into me being the bad guy!" I felt my voice wavering. "You're just like me, man."

He shook his head. "No, man, I wasn't just like you. I latched onto you. I looked up to you. I tried to be you, until I realized that being you wasn't shit."

I bit my lip. Breathed. "Alright, then. You said your piece. Can I go now?"

And this, for some reason, made Ollie bend over on the

couch, with his head in his hands. I felt like I was watching a man break down. Explode in on himself. "This is really it," he said. "This is really happening." He took another breath, wiped his eyes. "Okay, let's go. Let's take my car."

"Fine," I said.

In Ollie's car, I was simmering with fury. I kept trying to count the seconds, but couldn't. I couldn't focus. Ollie could tell. I wasn't as good at it as he was. "Here," he said, unfastening his watch. "Use this."

Feeling Ollie's warmth on the metal calmed me. I held out hope that he was my friend still, that we still had some form of connection that could be rekindled. I counted the seconds again, this time not losing track. Four seconds fast, just as always. I looked in the rear-view mirror, to see my guns in the backseat, and I held my breath to try and still my heart. I couldn't wait. I couldn't wait.

When Ollie parked, he looked at me with the saddest eyes I'd ever seen. "You can still turn back, for both of us."

"You know I can't," I said.

"Yeah," he said, weary. "I guess I knew that."

Ollie held his hands on the steering wheel, tight. His head hung low again. "Okay," he said. "Okay." He was crying. "Okay."

I thought of reaching out to touch him, to tell him it was going to be okay. That none of this would matter, but then he did something that surprised me entirely.

He took one hand off the steering wheel and thrust it down between his seat and the car door. A quick, sharp movement—maybe one he practiced. When his hand came out, he had a shiny black metal pistol.

I almost screamed in joy. "Oh God," I said. He was going to help me. Together. He couldn't resist, one last time as the Tide was high. "Fuck, man. How are we going to do it? One from one side, one from the back? One funnels them out into the killing field—that sort of thing?"

"No," he said. And that's when I noticed the gun was

pointed at me. His eyes were shiny. "There is no we, man. I'm sorry, man. I'm so, so sorry."

And I said: "But, why?"

"I'm cultivating my garden," he muttered.

And the gun kicked in his hand and the light flashed from the barrel and the slug hit me right in the gut and then I fell out of the car and I was just laughing, laughing my ass off, as the pain emanated from the wound and my stomach's acids burned against exposed nerves. I felt something horrible right then, that pain, as it finally hit me. Hit me like a train. But I was still laughing, alright. I was still laughing. "Jesus," I said. "You shot me. I thought it was my turn. I wanted my turn." And he was getting out of the car, circling it and coming for me, again. "You already had your turn. When's the next Tide, man? I can't do—shit, fuck, this hurt. I can't do shit like this."

He didn't say anything for a while, but somewhere near us, I heard a jogger scream. "He's got a gun!"

"Why she gotta be like that?" I asked. I wasn't mad though. I was losing lots of blood and soon I'd wake up in my own bed and I'd just have to do it again. Killing was better than dying, but I could do both, if I really wanted to. I was talented like that. "She's not supposed to care, right?"

"Right," he said.

"You think I'll die from the gut shot?" I said, and I was just lying there, letting death sweep me in its arms.

"Yeah, I think so," he said.

He had tucked his gun into his pants and was looking at his watch, staring at the seconds.

"When's the next Tide?" I asked, my voice faint.

"Yesterday," he said absently.

"Huh? Two in a row. Wow."

"No, not two in a row. Yesterday."

And I didn't quite get it, didn't quite get what he was saying, but he sat beside me on the asphalt, and he wiped tears from his eyes. "This is it," he said. "This is the end."

Somewhere, distantly, sirens blared and my vision went all fuzzy, so fuzzy that I could barely see Ollie putting the gun to his own head and I wanted to say something, like, "Hey, wait—you have to go inside, you have to blow Kev's brains out," and I think he knew I was going to say something like that because he just choked out the word, "No," and shook his head again.

Yeah, I was dying alright. I could feel everything that makes you alive fading away. I didn't like it, not really. But I appreciated it. It was different. Strange, new. It didn't feel like before. It felt so final. I wanted to tell Ollie about it, but all I could do was make motions with my lips. I just couldn't do shit. I couldn't move. I guessed that was how it went.

So, I just closed my eyes. I listened as the sirens got closer, louder—I lost myself in the bark of Ollie's pistol—and when he fell beside me, I thought about gardens and guns and death, everything—waiting to wake up.

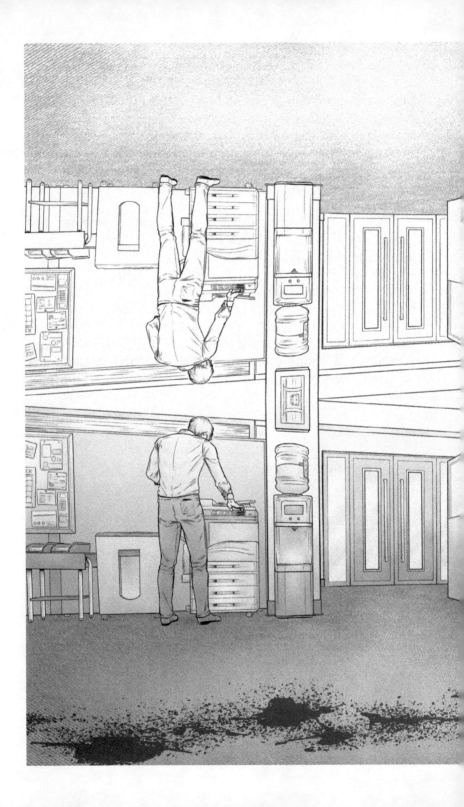

ACKNOWLEDGEMENTS

I wrote **Soft Targets** while working at a grocery store. Because of that, I think I have to thank the public for making this book possible. Good, bad, and ugly.

In its initial draft and beyond, many offered to beta read and provided me with excellent feedback. Thank you to Erik McHatton, who might be my biggest supporter—your enthusiasm keeps me going. Chris O'Halloran, thank you for reading and championing this book. Having you in my corner has made the journey into a dream. Thank you to RSL, who was always willing to read, laugh, and chat about class politics. And thank you to the wide, wild world of internet writing groups—there are too many of you to thank individually, but you know who you are. You continue to inspire me.

This book had an odd road to publication, but the fact that it's here at all is due to Matt and Alex. Thank you, sincerely. The work you put in is astounding and appreciated.

Finally, I'd like to thank my wife, Sarah. She has to listen to me talk about this stuff all the time and keeps the eye rolling to a minimum. I'm self-aware enough to know that that's harder than it sounds.

A NOTE FROM THE TENEBROUS PRESS TEAM

Although *Soft Targets* is not intended as a statement on gun violence in and of itself, there is no denying that the U.S. is in the critical stages of an ongoing catastrophe of its own devising; one that worsens year after year with no easy solution on the horizon.

We, the author and publisher, will be donating a portion of the proceeds of *Soft Targets* to **Sandy Hook Promise** (https://www.sandyhookpromise.org/) until such a time as such action is no longer necessary.

ABOUT THE CONTRIBUTORS

Carson Winter is a minimalist weirdo, a conversational absurdist, and a vehemently bleak-minded artist making his home in the Pacific Northwest. His fiction has appeared in *Vastarien, Apex,* and Dread Stone Press' *Split Scream* series. You can find him on Twitter @CarsonWinter3 or at carsonwinter.com.

Blacky Shepherd is a Pacific Northwest-based artist and writer, best known for his Horror collaborations with Cullen Bunn. He's also done work on *G.I. Joe* and *Transformers* for IDW Comics, and is currently working on a boutique toy line based on his original characters.

ABOUT TENEBROUS PRESS

Tenebrous Press was conceived in the Plague Year 2020 and unleashed, howling and feral, in spring 2021 to deliver the finest in transgressive, progressive Horror from diverse and unsung voices around the world.

We welcome the esoteric; the unorthodox; the finest in New Weird Horror.

FIND OUT MORE:
www.tenebrouspress.com
Twitter: @TenebrousPress

NEW WEIRD HORROR

CPSIA information can be obtained
at www.ICGtesting.com
Printed in the USA
JSHW080027180723
44871JS00005B/29